His Fantasy Maid

Susan Blexrud,
author of *The Gettysburg Vampire*

CRIMSON
ROMANCE
F+W Media, Inc.

This edition published by
Crimson Romance
an imprint of F+W Media, Inc.
10151 Carver Road, Suite 200
Blue Ash, Ohio 45242
www.crimsonromance.com

Copyright © 2013 by Susan Blexrud

ISBN 10: 1-4405-6351-9
ISBN 13: 978-1-4405-6351-5
eISBN 10: 1-4405-6352-7
eISBN 13: 978-1-4405-6352-2

Cover art © 123rf.com; istockphoto.com/Rouzes

Acknowledgments

As always, heartfelt gratitude goes to my incredible critique group, the Pink Fire Writers. Without the weekly input of Jeanne Charters, Beth Robrecht, and Sallie Bissell, I'd be a blundering writer in a sea of loneliness. They keep me sane.

Mounds of appreciation must be heaped on the lovely Mary Everett, whose experience as a nurse guided me through the emergency room and hospital scenes.

Finally, sincere thanks to Jennifer Lawler and the team at Crimson Romance, most particularly to Terese daly Ramin, my editor, who did an amazing job of spicy plumping (you know what I mean, girl).

Chapter One

Amy

If I believed the adage, "you are what you do," my self-concept would be in the toilet, so to speak. I clean houses in a bikini or French maid get-up, client's choice, which contributes little to making the world a better place. As a result, my adage is, "you are what you become," because I'm becoming a doctor.

But today, I'm Amy Maitland, fantasy maid.

My best friend and fellow medical resident, Ellen, knows about my undercover life working for Fantasy Maids, but she's the only one. If word got out at the College of Medicine, I'd be the laughingstock of the University of Central Florida. My five brothers know I work as a housemaid, which they respect as good, honest labor, but they don't know the fantasy aspect. Protective (and controlling) men that they are, they'd lock me up.

That said, it's not the worst job in the world. I've been a fantasy maid for almost two years; so far, none of my clients has tried to assault me. But it's always a possibility, considering Florida's propensity for perverts. The company (i.e. Rex, the owner and a part-time secretary) arms us with pepper spray and an emergency hotline number (Rex's cell phone), and they screen the customers to make sure no one's a registered sex offender. They also arrange our appointments and Rex is good about following up—within four or five days—to make sure we survived the gig.

Still, being alone with a strange guy in his apartment is enough to get anyone's adrenalin pumping and I never go into a new situation without first sending up a prayer. I always let Ellen know where I'm going and I carry a rosary, even though I'm not Catholic. A childhood friend gave me a strand of the rose-colored beads for Christmas one year, and they've been my protector ever since.

Today, I'm heading to a condominium in stylish Winter Park, just north of Orlando. The address alone is comforting. It's just off Park Avenue in a nice neighborhood next door to a church. But I remind myself Ted Bundy lived in a nice neighborhood. Let's face it: serial killers *can* look like the boy next door.

My old, white Honda sputters into the church parking lot adjacent to the condominium complex without any signs of cardiac arrest (this I take as a good omen). The Rambling Waters sign on the wrought iron gate looks welcoming.

I turn off the ignition and my ancient car heaves a sigh. Grabbing my backpack with my stash of costumes, I hop out of my car and punch in the security code at the entrance gate. It creaks open like the sound at the beginning of Michael Jackson's Thriller, which my brother Matt plays ad nauseam around Halloween.

As I enter the property, I notice a network of ponds meandering around the buildings. I'm sure the landscape architect intended them to be beautiful, but all I see is a maintenance nightmare—all that algae to eradicate. I shake my head. I've been cleaning too long.

I nod to an elderly couple walking their white miniature poodle. The dog is decked out in a purple vest and ear bows and looks slightly embarrassed. Good to know I'm not the only one who wears ridiculous outfits.

"Can we help you find something, dear?" the woman inquires. Could it be because I'm standing here with the address in one hand and a blank stare on my face?

We're supposed to look inconspicuous when we arrive at a job so the casual witness doesn't get wigged out by a neighbor's proclivities. To that end, I'm dressed in my usual jeans and t-shirt. Would she call me dear if she saw me in uniform?

My appointment is for six P.M. and I'm already a few minutes late. I count seven buildings on the property, with no visible numbers. Gratefully, I say, "Thank you. I'm looking for unit Five B."

The woman elbows her companion. "Oh, that's where that nice young lawyer lives. What's his name, Harold?"

Harold shrugs and the woman pulls her poodle away from the geranium it's been nibbling on. She cups one hand around her mouth and points to Harold with the other. "He's not very observant." She rolls her eyes. "Building Five is just to the right of the pool, which is straight ahead."

"Thanks." I head in the direction she indicates. My sandals crunch as pavement gives way to gravel. I look down to find strategically-placed stepping stones in the shape of turtles. Strategically placed for Big Foot, that is. The stones are way too far apart for my five-foot-three leg span. I essentially hurtle from turtle to turtle, using my backpack for ballast. I'm working up a sweat in the May humidity.

Behind me the woman calls out, "Spending the night?"

It's none of her business either way, but when you reach a certain age, you don't mince words. I find that endearing. It's one of the reasons I'm leaning toward a specialty in geriatrics. I stifle a smile and leap on like I don't hear her.

I count twenty turtles by the time I find Five B, which is on the second floor. I squint into the partly cloudy sky and cross myself before I start up the steps to indulge the imagination of my latest employer. My sandals slap the stairs; the flat surface is comforting after the series of round turtle backs.

My nerves always wait until the last possible moment to go bonkers and, as I'm standing at the door poised to rap, my heart begins to pound so loudly I'm not sure I even need to knock. Rex promotes his fantasy maids as being "doe-eyed and dewy" when he talks with potential clients—"doe-eyed and dewy" being the equivalent of virginally innocent. Today, though, between rushing to get here, the turtle stepping stones, and the flight of stairs, I'm more drenched than dewy, which is not exactly the sexy image I'm supposed to project. Still, for better or worse, this is Florida where heat and humidity go hand in hand, meaning that if you exert yourself at all, "drenched" is to be expected. It must be ninety degrees. I dab at my face with my t-shirt then fan my hands under my arms to get a breeze going. I hope my deodorant holds up.

Okay, show time.

As my fingers reach for the claddagh knocker on the front door, I spot the doorbell and opt for that instead. The chime rings the theme from *Doctor Zhivago*. As it happens, my mom's favorite movie, God rest her soul. I'm caught off-guard and tears well up. I'm swiping at my eyes when the door opens.

The guy across the threshold presses a finger to his lips and pulls me into the condominium. He sort of props me next to the wall. "You don't have a cold, do you? If you do, I want a discount." He backs away and eyes me up and down then he grins. "Good old Claudia would shit a brick if she saw you."

"I take it I won't be meeting good old Claudia?" I shiver from the blast of air conditioning, though it's welcome relief.

"Hell, no, she's the fiancée…and my sister. Stay right here. Don't move." He takes off down a hall.

"Uh, okay." Wherever this is going, all I can think is how grateful I am for the cool air. I rub my arms and glance around the uncluttered, tasteful living room. It's immaculately decorated in beige and chocolate brown, strong masculine colors. I can't imagine what I'm going to clean.

As I'm sizing up the job, another guy emerges from the hallway. One towel wraps around his tight-as-a-drum middle as he dries his hair with another. My jaw drops. I almost have to push it closed. Six feet, wavy dark brown hair, and broad shoulders…my dream formula. My belly tightens and I get a little twinge…below my umbilicus.

"Whoa, pardon me," he says as he tosses his hair towel to his friend and tightens the one around his waist. "I didn't know we were expecting company."

"Surprise!" his friend bellows, clapping Mr. Gorgeous on the back. "She's an early bachelor party gift. Your groomsmen, yours truly included, decided to loosen you up a bit before we head to the strip club. May I introduce your fantasy maid?"

Oh, no, my least favorite client (aside from a rapist, of course) is the fellow who gets a fantasy maid as a gift. There's inevitably time wasted while everyone has a good laugh. Well, not everyone laughs. The tricksters do. The trickee typically hems and haws and turns ten shades of red. But the tricksters always prevail. They've paid for the service and by God they're going to ensure that some cleaning gets done.

This is where I ask, "Do you have a room where I can change and would you like the bikini or the French maid outfit?" Today I'm kind of wishing I'd brought another outfit to suggest, as in one that might fulfill my own fantasies where this particular client is concerned. Although, the towel he's wearing with nothing under it is working pretty well—if I let it, which…I really shouldn't. Besides, after working up a sweat outside, I've got goose bumps from the air conditioning that make me wish guys fantasized about fur-clad Eskimos cleaning their apartments.

Of course, maybe my goose pimples are a sign of something else, like the sight of this yummy man.

"Look, Miss…what's your name?" This from Mr. Gorgeous, who looks my age or a few years older. He extends one hand for a handshake, holding fast to his towel with the other. I wonder if he's ticklish.

I place my hand in his. Warm fingers wrap around mine. Very nice. "I'm Amy, your fantasy maid." My voice is at least an octave higher than usual. His eyes grow wide. I guess he wasn't expecting me to squeak. Clearing my throat, I launch into my shtick. "I'm here for two hours to provide anything you need in the way of cleaning. I even do windows." I display a toothy grin. What is wrong with me?

"Well, I'm Jake. And while I appreciate the generosity of my groomsmen," he looks at his friend and mock-growls, "you don't need to stick around to do my cleaning." He smiles and I swear his eyes twinkle.

I melt. I'm staring into his green (my favorite color) eyes and I have a compelling urge to brush the hair off his brow and step closer. If his embrace is as warm as his handshake…stop it. Also, he's just had a shower. He smells like sandalwood. I want to lick him. I shake my head…and my thoughts. Back to work. As Rex says in our Fantasy Maid Manual, "When the client is reluctant, press on…with finesse."

"So, French maid or bikini?"

"I'd go for the bikini," his friend pipes in. "And if you take her up on the windows, I'll get the ladder. Bet the view is great."

Yuck! But I act professional, even in this most unprofessional situation. "Just so you know the rules, there's no touching." As I look back at Jake, I'm thinking I should have kept my mouth shut. I want to run my hands down that washboard stomach. Stop that. "I clean and you're welcome to watch. This is a cleaning service, not an escort service."

"That's good to know," Jake says. I see the wheels turning in that beautiful head of his. He seems to be softening. He shrugs. Bingo. "Tell you what, my dishwasher needs to be unloaded and you can make my bed and straighten up in the bedroom. Do you iron?"

"Yes, sir, I do. In fact, I love to iron." Phew, a task. Nothing like a task to tamp down the hormones.

"Great, there are a few shirts hanging above the dryer in the laundry room. The board's in a narrow closet and the iron is in the cabinet above the sink. And please don't call me sir."

I nod. This guy is organized. It's a great combination, gorgeous and organized. "So, if you'll just show me where I can change?"

His friend (still don't know his name, but the one who's doing this for *his sister's* fiancé?) rubs his hands together. "Oh, boy."

"It's not necessary for you to change," Jake says. "Just do the tasks. I'm sure you'll earn whatever Sam has paid you."

Now I know his name, Sam…rhymes with Spam.

"No way," says Sam. "This may be a gift for you, but I paid for it. I'm going to enjoy it, even if I don't get the ladder view."

Men can be so adolescent. I blink a few times to keep from rolling my eyes. That would be unprofessional. "Part of the contract is that you get a photo of me in my get-up. The boss doesn't like it when we don't come back with a photo. He says his photo album is a great marketing tool." Oh, geez, it sounds like I'm describing a pimp.

"He sounds obnoxious," Jake says.

"Heavens, no, he's not. Rex is a sweetheart." Now it sounds like he's my boyfriend. I'm batting zero. I need a moment alone. "I'll just slip into the bathroom and change. Since Sam's lobbied for the bikini…" It's just as well since I paid thirty dollars for a wax yesterday. I ease past Jake and head for the bathroom. When I close the door, the mirrors are still fogged and the scent of sandalwood wafts from the shower. I close my eyes and breathe in the spicy scent, imagining Jake's hands all over my body, soaping from my quadriceps up. My hands creep to my breasts. I pretend my hands are his…and pinch my nipples. Oh, geez, I could go a long way with this. What if Jake were to slip into the bathroom right about now? He'd wrap an arm around my waist and ease me forward over the vanity. His thick rod would press against my back. He'd sort of roll it around my butt, and that's when I'd take the not so subtle hint and bend deeper over the counter. He'd slip a hand between my legs and find my bud, which by this time would be throbbing. Oh, great Scot, the juices are starting to flow. Maybe I can just rub my legs together for a few minutes and ...

Earth to Amy! This is so *not* like me. I don't believe in instant attraction, at least, not until now. I press my thumbs into my eye sockets, pressure points for a reality check. My brain fart must be due to lack of sleep and too many anatomical charts. I remind myself of the no fraternizing rule, which if I recall, is number nine in the Fantasy Maid Manual. Besides, this guy's engaged. As I pull my t-shirt over my head and unzip my jeans, I think back to my previous job as a theme park hotel maid. No costumes, but the hours didn't work with school and the money barely covered the cost of gas to get there. Yep, this job has made all the difference in paying for my education. I don't know how else I could have realized my dream.

By the time I've positioned the bottom triangle of my bikini and made sure the top provides as much coverage as a few inches of spandex allow, I fluff my bangs and salute my mirror image. I'm tingling all over. I'm usually a bit jittery at this point in the gig anyway. The unveiling (that would be me in costume) and the subsequent client reaction can be unnerving. But today I'm beyond nerves. I take a few cleansing breaths. As the manual emphasizes, "Be sexy and be strong."

Chapter Two

Jake

Damn, I nicked my chin. I press a cotton ball to the cut and scowl at myself in the mirror. Clearly my nerves are frayed. I've always hated bachelor parties. Here I'm promising to love, honor, and cherish Claudia for the rest of my life, and Sam's conniving libido comes up with a fantasy maid to set the night of debauchery in motion. And wouldn't you know she'd be beyond hot. I've never nicked my chin over Claudia.

Besides being hot, the girl, Amy, looks so wholesome. What's she doing in a job like this? I check to make sure my chin's stopped bleeding then head into the bedroom to get dressed.

It takes me a while to choose what to wear. Not sure why, since everything in my closet is navy. Popular psychology suggests juries are more sympathetic to lawyers in blue. I wonder what would happen if one day I ran amok and wore brown. I pick one of my striped shirts and pair it with, big surprise, navy slacks. I put on my glasses, the new tortoise shell designer frames Claudia gave me for Christmas. She says they make me look like an English barrister. I think they make me look like the geek I am.

When I enter the living room, Amy, who's talking with Sam, turns. She must have heard my heart thud. A body like that shouldn't be legal. From the tip of her strawberry blonde ponytail, to her gracefully sloping shoulders, full breasts spilling out of that miniscule top, and derriere luscious as a ripe apricot, she's physical perfection. And, unless there's something hidden beneath the tiny triangles masquerading as a bikini, not one tattoo mars the gorgeous skin covering her petite frame. I need to sit down. I may be drooling…like my dad's bloodhound. I take off my glasses and pitch them on the couch. A bit of blur might do me good.

"Hey, buddy, you look like you could use a beer." Sam clamps a hand on my shoulder and steers me to the kitchen. He pushes me onto a stool at the counter.

I hear Amy's little cat feet padding behind. She enters the kitchen and hands me my glasses. "Most accidents happen at home," she says. "You'd be surprised how many people get injured simply because they neglect to wear their glasses or contacts in familiar surroundings."

Oh, God, that sounded like something I'd say. Reluctantly, I put my glasses back on. I was going to tell her to start in the laundry room, but when she heads for the dishwasher and bends over the lower rack, I don't have the strength to talk. I want to close the distance between us, sink to my knees and circle her belly button with my tongue.

"Here, chug this," Sam says, offering a beer. "I'll admit you couldn't Photoshop a better body, but you'll get used to it once you've had a gulp or two. I'm on my third tall one and the numbness helps. It's like visiting the Grand Canyon. At first you're overwhelmed then all that mountain majesty starts looking the same."

I nod at Amy. Under my breath, I stage whisper to Sam, "I don't think *those* peaks and valleys are anything I'd ever get used to."

Amy spreads two kitchen towels on the counter. "I hope you're using the high heat setting on your dishwasher. It's not as energy efficient as a lower temperature, but it's the only setting that will kill germs."

She starts propping wine glasses upside down on the towels. "You can get a rinsing agent for the dishwasher that helps with spots on the glasses," she says. "Otherwise, you forever have to wipe them off." She takes another towel and begins rubbing a glass. What did she say? I'm finding it hard to focus. I watch her hands and the way they caress the crystal. I want her to caress me, to run her fingers through my hair, to press those glorious breasts against my chest.

Sam laughs. "I think the only spots are in front of Jake's eyes." He waves his hands in front of my face. "Drink up. We've got a big night ahead. Club Juana awaits."

I'm behaving like an idiot and moving like a zombie with lead feet. Where did the crack litigator go, the man who never succumbs to nerves? Concentrate on the woman I'm getting ready to marry. What's her name, again? Just kidding. Claudia. She has it all... intelligence, looks, and a great sense of humor. Maybe she isn't tops in the compassion department: she rides her employees pretty hard. No, that isn't fair. She's charitable in her way. I just wonder whether she contributes to causes more for the business it might bring her boutique than out of a sense of compassion. I chug my beer and push away from the table. "I need to, uh, pick a tie for tonight." I stagger to my bedroom. I seem to have lost my coordination.

Bracing my hands on the dresser, I stare in the large mirror, willing my heart rate back to normal. And then I see Amy's reflection behind me. Maybe I need a defibrillator.

"I'm done in the kitchen. May I make your bed?" she inquires.

Not before we mess it up some more. "Oh, sure." My voice is as hoarse as I sound after coaching the Winter Park Little League. I ease myself, hand-over-hand, to the closet, careful not to look at her on the way. Once there, I thumb through the ties absentmindedly. I choose a purple polka dot. I consider it a brave decision, sort of like ordering eel at a sushi restaurant.

"Whoa, that's an interesting choice," Amy says as I dangle the tie in front of her. I believe her eyes cross. "I'll put this as delicately as I can...are you color blind?"

I glance at the tie then at my blue and yellow-striped shirt. "I've never had trouble before. Maybe it's a virus?"

"Sorry to break this news, but color blindness is a genetic mutation. No cure. Did you think the color blind germ lurks in closets, waiting to pounce on vulnerable males?" She laughs.

She has no idea *how* vulnerable this male is. "Yeah, something like that. Maybe I could use some help with a tie selection?" Oh, no, why did I suggest that? Close proximity here we come. My stomach tightens.

"Gladly," she says, easing past me and into the closet, but not before her breasts graze my shirt. I don't think she intended to brush me. Her breasts are just so...there. And the hitch in my pants is just so there, too. I follow her into the closet.

"Let's see." She sifts through my tie rack, looking back at my shirt, which surely sports sweat rings by now. She nibbles on her bottom lip. She should stop that. I could do it better. I try to recall my multiplication tables as her gaze drifts over me—er, my ensemble—and the hitch in my pants gathers momentum.

Please, don't look lower.

Her eyes travel down my torso, grow wide then quickly pop back to my face, which is surely purple...from embarrassment.

With a rigid arm, she holds out a navy blue paisley tie. "This one is nice. The trick is to start with the predominant color in the shirt then make it fun. And here's another one." She brandishes a tie with diagonal stripes. "You might not think you could use diagonal stripes with a striped shirt, but as long as the stripes are different sizes, like a two-to-one ratio, it can be dramatic." She leans in and squints at my shirt. Oh, God, I want to kiss her. "Your shirt stripes are about one-quarter inch apart and the stripes on this tie are at least one-half inch apart, so that works." She looks up at me. "You're staring like I'm from outer space."

If she comes one silly millimeter closer, she'll feel my erection. I back up. "Do you moonlight as a fashion consultant?" A bead of sweat trickles down between my eyes and dangles from my nose.

I take the paisley tie from her lovely hands and, without thinking, wipe my nose with it. Now, that's couth.

She laughs. "Okay, so I guess that means the stripes win. My grandfather owned a haberdashery in downtown Orlando. I used to spend a lot of time there when I was growing up. He taught me all I know about ties. He was a fashion visionary, combining stripes as early as the 1960s, which was way before I was born."

God, she's even prettier when she laughs. "Haberdashery? There's a word you don't hear much anymore."

"Yeah, there aren't many of them left. It's sad, isn't it? Our country was founded on small business and entrepreneurship, and now we're all about Wal-Mart. I hate to see so many small businesses fail."

Oh, great, she's got a heart, too. I have to get out of this closet. She smells like the roses in my mother's garden. Another second and I'll bury my nose in her hair. I back up—directly into my row of suit jackets. The rack falls to the floor and I tumble down with it. Plunked on my rear and draped with jackets, I glance up at her. She leans down. Cleavage like that belongs in Wikipedia… the ultimate definition. I want to bury my face in her breasts and happily suffocate there. This has to end. "Oh, please, straighten up. My heart's about to give out."

She laughs, again. So cute.

"I'll just head to the laundry room," she says. "I'll finish up in the bedroom, later."

Or we'll finish up in the bedroom. I have clearly lost my mind.

• • •

Amy

I scoot out of the closet as fast as I can. What has gotten into me? The cardinal rule of the service is not to share any personal information with the client and here I've told him about my grandfather's store. He could Google "Downtown Orlando in the 1960s," and he'd probably learn all about Maitland's…and my family. He might even connect the dots to me. He'd find out everything about me, including that I've just started my residency at Orlando Regional Medical Center and that three of my brothers are professional football players. Well, facing down linebackers might be a deterrent.

Wait a minute, let's be realistic. Jake's engaged. He's going to his bachelor party tonight, which means that the wedding is soon, possibly even this weekend. My heart thuds. I wish I'd met him before he proposed to Claudia. Yep, timing in life is everything and my timing is notoriously off.

I almost leaped into his arms in the closet when I saw the bulge in his slacks. Yes, we're supposed to be provocative, but I violated a rule in the Fantasy Maid Manual: "Maintain eye contact and never look down." Dagnabbit. I was more professional than this.

Okay, I'm in the laundry room. Time to ignore the throbbing between my legs and get to work. Iron, check; ironing board, check; distilled water for steam iron, check; spray starch, check; four shirts hanging above the dryer, check. I'm ready to get started. Maybe I'll just sneak one of his shirts home so I can sleep in it, like I did with my boyfriend's football jersey in high school. Oh, God, I'm regressing. Please, please don't come in here, Jake.

I truly do enjoy ironing. When I was growing up, my grandfather let me use the pants press in the back of his store. I loved the sizzling sound it made when the steam escaped and how the pants came out perfectly creased, though the starch on the material sometimes made my head swim. Like my head's swimming now. Get to work.

I'm ironing and humming "Somewhere, My Love," when Jake appears in the doorway. He's in a fresh shirt. It's in a stripe similar to his other shirt, so it still goes with the tie. I want to capture his image in my mind's eye and keep it there forever. He catches my perusal.

"I, uh, got a little hot in the closet and needed to change," he says, ducking his head a bit.

I have nothing to say to that—except—*Please, leave*, which I keep to myself.

"I'm concerned about you ironing with essentially no clothes on," he says. "What if you burn yourself? People have sued for less. After the fast-food coffee case, you might even sue me." He smiles.

"Not to worry, I'm a doc...I mean, I'm experienced with this." Oops. I blow my bangs out of my eyes. They've gotten a bit damp.

"You're a doctor?"

"No, no, of course not, I was just reminded of a joke I heard on late night television. It had something to do with anatomy... or ironing...or Conan O'Brien." I'm blithering. I never watch late night television, but I can't think of anything else to distract myself from what I want him to do to me—or let me do to him. The urge to suck on a certain part of his anatomy is so overwhelming that I want to scream. I puff out my cheeks like a blowfish and turn my attention back to the ironing board. I gaze at the cuffs I'm working on and spritz them with a healthy dose of spray starch.

"You may not be a doctor, but you're certainly a lot more than a fantasy maid."

I stop ironing. Bad mistake. He leans over the ironing board. His lips come at me like a torpedo in transit and I'm the enemy submarine. But instead of a collision, his lips are oh, so soft when they meet mine. He traces a slow journey inside my bottom lip with his tongue and I can't help but moan. He takes my face in his hands and I spread my fingers over his solid chest. His pectoral muscles flex and I feel his heartbeat. It's racing. This is the best kiss of my life and, oh, I want it to last. He tastes like nothing I've ever experienced, like he gargled with a mouthwash called "Sexy Man." I ease my hands up his chest and behind his neck where my fingers on the prickly little hairs above his collar make us both shiver. Oh, the wonders of human anatomy. My nerve endings are firing like a machine gun. My pulse pounds. My heart rate matches his. I quickly go through a mental list of the symptoms of atrial fibrillation: light-headedness—yes; palpitations—yes; fatigue—no! I'm ready for a kissing marathon. My toes curl.

Is smoke coming out of my ears? Something's burning. I pull back from his embrace and glance down at the ironing board. I left the iron on his shirt.

"Criminy!" I yank the iron off the board, grab the scorched shirt, and plunge it into the sink. Not that water will do anything at this point, but it might at least dissipate the smell of singed fabric. "I can't believe I did that. I haven't scorched a shirt since I was ten years old." I turn from the sink and narrow my eyes at Jake. "But it was your fault."

"I am so sorry. I don't know what got into me. Please, just…" He throws up his hands and seems to be contemplating the incandescent bulbs in the ceiling. "On second thought, I'm sorry for taking that liberty, but I'm not really sorry for kissing you." He looks back at me, a sheepish grin on his face.

"If you must know, me neither." I have definitely violated rule number six of the Fantasy Maid Manual, which states that we must at all times preserve a margin of personal space of ten inches or more. I gaze into his eyes. My throat constricts. I take a deep breath and choose my words carefully. "I'm sure you're not yourself this evening. You probably realize that your days of kissing girls you're not married to are numbered and grabbed for a little gusto. Perhaps it's best if you have a seat on the couch in the living room. I'll just finish up and be on my way."

He runs a hand through that gorgeous head of hair. "The wedding's in two weeks, but I'm not the kind of guy that 'grabs for gusto,' as you put it. I wanted to kiss you. I did it. I don't know what came over me. You told me the rule is no touching and I'm not a rule breaker." The corners of his mouth turn down. I want to do something to make him smile because I know how he feels. He's both disappointed in himself and possibly wondering what made him act so compulsively. He's a straight arrow, like me.

"Don't be too hard on yourself. Fantasy maids are supposed to be tantalizing. It's encouraged in our manual. It doesn't mean you won't be a good husband."

"Hey, what're you guys doing in here?" Sam appears in the doorway and focuses on my work-in-progress. "I once had sex on an ironing board."

"Where haven't you had sex, Sam?" Jake asks.

Sam taps a finger to his temple. "Let's see, the most unusual places? On a flight to Rio I became a member of the Mile High Club with a hot Hispanic stewardess. And then there was the time in the Keys when things got pretty kinky with the scuba instructor while I was diving." Sam laughs. "I don't advise sex in a wet suit. It's messy."

I swear, Jake blushes. "Too much information. Sorry I asked." He shakes his head. "Come on, Sam. Let's get going before you say something else to embarrass yourself."

"I'm not embarrassed." Sam shrugs, then he follows Jake to the living room.

I need to wrap things up here, but before I change back into my jeans and t-shirt, I've got the obligatory photo to do. I tidy up the laundry room and scoot past the fellows in the living room. Grabbing my digital camera from the front pocket of my backpack, I return to the living room and hand it to Sam. "If you wouldn't mind doing the honors?"

"Sure." He takes the camera and motions for me to join Jake on the couch. "How about you put your hand on her thigh, Jake?"

Jake sits stiffly and leans away from me like I have leprosy. He doesn't put his hand on my thigh. I knew he wouldn't and I'm glad. That kiss was a moment of madness and neither of us wants another temptation. I settle next to him, but not too close.

"You two look like you're ready for the firing squad. Can't you smile?" Sam raises the camera to his face.

Jake and I glance at each other then turn our attention to the camera. I don't know if he's smiling, but I hear a small sigh.

"Okay, if that's the best you can do." Sam does his duty and hands me the camera, along with his card. "Send me a copy for my refrigerator."

I take the camera and card. "Will do." I hurry to the bedroom. I can't get back into my street clothes fast enough. I nick my finger as I zip up my jeans. It's no wonder, since I'm trembling. As I practically race through the living room to the front door, Sam intervenes.

"Don't you want to get paid?" He chuckles.

I shoot a glance to Jake, who rises slowly from the couch. He's getting up to be polite. That's the kind of guy he is. The look of sheer confusion on his face tells me he's as anxious to get this over with as I am. I look back at Sam, who's offering me an envelope. Did he take up a collection?

I take it from his hand, but not before he does the little cat and mouse thing where he pulls it away a few times before he lets me keep it. So not amusing.

"Thanks." I open the door then look back at Jake. "Good luck with your wedding. I wish you every happiness."

I'm trembling as I walk to my car. I'm always glad when I finish a job, but it's usually because a girl can only stand so much lascivious gawking. Today I'm just relieved to be away from someone I wanted to curl up with. Back to reality, Amy. Another few months of this job and I'll have enough saved to pay off my student loans. Before I start my car, I open the envelope Sam gave me. Three crisp fifties. Where else could a girl make this kind of money with such flexible hours? Well, there's the world's oldest profession, but I'm not going there.

Then I look at the picture Sam took on my camera. The nicest guy I've ever met looks back at me. And he's taken.

Chapter Three

Jake

Claudia bursts into my office unannounced. "Darling, please don't tell me you have to work late tonight." Her lilting soprano could shatter glass.

I turn from my computer, where I've been looking at the photo Sam forwarded of me and Amy. Before I can minimize the screen, Claudia's eagle eyes fix on the image.

"Ah, so this is the little tart who cleaned your apartment. Considering the photo as your screen saver?" She puts a hand on my shoulder and digs in her fingernails as she squints at the image. "She *is* attractive, but it seems like overkill by your groomsmen. Didn't the strip club provide enough bump and grind for one evening?"

A strong urge to defend Amy grips my gut. "She was actually a very nice girl. You can't lump all the guys in with Sam. He's the mastermind."

"I doubt his mind had much to do with this prank. Knowing Sam, more basic instincts ruled his decision."

"Well, he's *your* brother. You should be used to his schemes." I glance back at the screen. "You'll notice that I'm not looking too happy." More like miserable…and sad.

Claudia begins massaging my shoulders. "My poor darling, you don't like surprises, do you? And in my family, we live for them. I'll just have to become more moderate for my staid husband."

She bends to my ear and begins a slow nibble. Usually, this raises my temperature, but today it's just irritating.

"Keep that up and I'll never get my work done."

"Work? Seems to me you were taking a break."

"Just checking e-mails for a moment." I minimize the photo, but not before I steal another glance. I take off my glasses. Claudia in full focus can be intense.

She gives me one last neck rub. "Oh, all right. Mr. Lawyer isn't into any mischief this afternoon. And just when I was in the mood for some desktop delight." She shrugs. "I suppose I'll be on my way. But remember, my parents are hosting us at the club at seven. Can you pick me up or shall we meet there?"

Claudia fiddles with the multiple bracelets on her arm. It's usually a cute habit, but this afternoon something about it grates on my nerves. The bracelets clang like cow bells. I tell myself it's nothing—I'm just very busy. "Let's meet there. I doubt I'll get out of here before six-thirty."

"Okay, you hunka hunka burning love." Claudia flicks her manicured finger over my chin. "I'll have a martini waiting for you at the bar, so don't be late."

That's Claudia's little trick to make me punctual. She thinks I'd jump over the judge's desk to avoid a warm martini, but honestly, I'm not that picky. And I prefer beer.

She blows me a kiss over her shoulder as she practically bolts out of my office, leaving the scent of Coco by Chanel in her wake. I know the name because she wrote it down for me last Christmas. The woman lives her life on high alert. Between her and Sam, it's a contest for who can generate the most drama.

Looking ahead a few years, I hope motherhood will calm her down. I dream of sitting in the bleachers, watching my son play football, or beaming as our daughter pirouettes across the stage at her ballet recital. Well, that was stereotypical. Maybe the roles will be reversed. Anything's possible. I'm sure Claudia will have our children dressed to the nines, whatever the occasion. Oh, no, I just flashed on an image of our five-year-old son in a Hugh Hefner smoking jacket. That's scary.

I turn back to my computer, put my glasses back on, and maximize the image of Amy and me again. I allow myself one last glimpse at her lovely face. I can't help smiling, remembering her advice about choosing ties. I start to delete the picture, but don't. The hint of her smile is soothing. I save it in my "friends" folder.

• • •

Amy

In the big uniform supply closet, Ellen pitches me a clean pair of scrubs. "So, how was your latest trick?"

Good thing we're the only ones here, though I hear voices close by.

"Keep your voice down," I say, covering my mouth with my finger, "and he was hardly a trick." I smile then quickly suck in my cheeks, but I'm not quick enough for Ellen.

"Hold on. A smile? I'm used to a shudder. Was this guy half normal?"

"More than normal. He was perfect. Honestly, he was everything I've ever wanted in a man—handsome, sexy, funny, and very nice. I wish I'd met him under other circumstances." Heat prickles my cheeks. They're probably turning red and I curse myself for being so transparent.

Ellen's eyes grow wide. "Maybe you could go back to his apartment and say you lost an earring or something. Surely you could bypass Rex's no-fraternizing rule in the interest of kismet."

"No way, Ellen, but that's not the main reason. Jake's getting married in a couple of weeks. He's looming large in someone else's future." Ellen and I take our scrubs to the small changing room off the residents' lounge. For the month of June, we're working third shift ER. "Love is the last thing I'm looking for. There'll be plenty of time for a man in my life once I'm in practice."

"Yeah, those fellows in the nursing home will be prime candidates." Ellen chuckles. "You might find a rich widower with a bad cough."

I press a hand to my heart. "I'll save him for you." I laugh, but a niggling emptiness gnaws at my gut. Timing in life is everything and fate has botched my timing with Jake.

"Please don't." Ellen's eyebrows almost meet in the middle, a sure sign she's mulling something over. "But if you're feeling magnanimous, you might put in a good word to one of your brothers. Honestly, I don't care which one. They're all gorgeous."

"Oh, Lord, be careful whom you covet. They may be cute, but they're a controlling lot."

"That's because you were the little sister. They feel duty bound to keep you in line. I, on the other hand, would be the little sister's sexy, wait amend that to *very* sexy, friend."

"I knew it was a mistake to introduce you to them."

"Well, duh, it was graduation." Ellen rolled her eyes. "You had to introduce your best friend to your family."

I can't help myself; I do a full body shiver, like Freddie Kreuger just stepped into the supply closet. "All through high school, I never knew whether girls wanted to be friends because they liked me or lusted after my brothers."

"You can't lump me in with them. You know I love ya and I didn't even know about your brothers until we were already friends."

I sigh and then shrug. "Okay, I'll see what Matt's up to. He's the least intimidating. Not a lot upstairs, but as long as you've got your wits about you, you should be fine."

"You mean I could be in danger?"

I chuckle. "Not intentionally, but Matt once sat on grandma and almost crushed her. She was little anyway, but when she hunkered down in a big wing chair, he didn't see her and he collapsed his two-hundred-fifty pounds onto her. She's ninety pounds soaking wet."

"You must take after your grandma. I couldn't believe the size of your brothers and you're like five-foot-three."

"Yeah, I'm grateful for that. Not that I wouldn't like a few inches, but six-foot-five could be limiting."

"Not if you wanted to play basketball." Ellen beamed. "Now, get on the phone and call Matt."

• • •

Jake

By the time I look up from the brief I'm poring over, it's seven o'clock. Crap! I'll miss rush hour traffic on Interstate 4, but even if I use valet at Orlando Country Club, it will still take twenty minutes to get there. I fly out of the office. Most of the commuters have left for the day, so at least I don't have to wait to exit the garage. My old BMW purrs at the stoplight before the interstate entrance ramp.

Claudia wants me to get a fancy car befitting my new partner status, but I'm attached to Olde Bleu. I bought him used when I graduated from law school and with monumental student loans to re-pay, I just made the final payment on him a few months ago. Claudia's embarrassed to ride in Olde Bleu, so we usually take her new silver Mercedes, though it's a bit glitzy for my taste. I wonder what kind of car Amy drives. I picture her in a lime green Volkswagen Beetle. Get a grip.

I merge into steady traffic, glad I've missed the bumper-to-bumper scene that typically dissipates around six forty-five. It's busier in the opposite direction. Must be an Orlando Magic home game tonight. I pass the Ivanhoe exit, knowing I need to get into the right lane to exit at Princeton when a van heading in the opposite direction slams into the concrete median.

Oh, shit!

Chapter Four

Amy

Ellen and I wait outside for the first ambulance to arrive. A car crash with casualties means the sore throats, sprained ankles, and impacted bowels lined up in the ER will have to wait. We're Central Florida's only Level One Trauma Center, so the most serious emergencies typically come here. We rush forward as the ambulance careens into the bay. Paramedics leap out of the vehicle and begin briefing us as they unload the injured.

"Thirty-year-old white male, possible cracked ribs, no obvious contusions, no loss of blood. The steering wheel slammed into his chest, so his breathing's pretty erratic. We put on a cervical collar to keep him immobilized. No medical allergies. Started a saline and dextrose IV and hooked him to a heart monitor. His pulse and blood pressure are slightly elevated. He's in a lot of pain, but I couldn't give him any morphine with his shallow respirations."

"Didn't the air bag inflate?" Ellen asks.

"Older car."

"Where to, Dr. Maitland?" The EMT asks after glancing at my name tag.

"Let's get him to X-ray to take a look at those ribs." I look at Ellen. "We'll do an ultrasound to check for internal bleeding and we should make sure the OR is available just in case." I bend over the patient to check his pupils for shock.

"Oh, God, I know this man." I look at Ellen. "It's Jake." My heart kicks into overdrive and I prickle with gooseflesh. A wave of nausea freezes me to the pavement.

"Your trick?" Ellen clamps a hand over her mouth. "I mean your, uh, friend?"

I nod, or rather jerk, my head up and down a few times. My hands are clammy as I grip the rails of the gurney, but this is no time to panic. I take a deep breath then Ellen and I sprint through the double glass doors and into the vestibule of the ER. God, please let him be all right. I pat my pocket, wishing I had my rosary. We race down the hall to where a triage nurse waves us into an examining room.

Jake moans.

"Don't move him until we check the X-rays." I motion to a Certified Nursing Assistant, who hurries down the hall to alert the X-ray technician. "Hang in there. I know it hurts to breathe."

Jake opens his eyes to my voice. And then his eyes get bigger. "Am I dead?" He squints hard at me. Maybe he won't recognize me without his glasses.

My heart's still in my throat, but I cough out a chuckle. He's responsive. "No, you're going to be fine."

"I must be dead. You wouldn't be here unless I was dead. You're my angel."

One of the EMTs shakes his head. "Trauma can do strange things to people."

"He must have liked you as much as you liked him," Ellen says across the gurney.

I look down at Jake, whose gorgeous face is twisted with pain. "You've had an automobile accident. You're in shock. We're going to take a few X-rays and do an ultrasound to see the extent of the damage. You may have cracked a rib or two." I feel tears welling. That will never do. I blink them back.

His pained expression doesn't fade. "What's on my neck?"

I touch his shoulder gently. "It's a cervical collar. The EMTs put it on to keep you immobilized. We won't be able to remove it until we take a look at the X-rays."

I can see him rolling this information around as he squints up at me. "You're still not real," he says.

I'm always empathetic to the plight of an accident victim, but this is more than that. This isn't a nameless victim, it's Jake. And he's hurting. My heart aches for him.

We put him in the X-ray lab and wait a few minutes while the technician positions the portable machine we use for patients who are unable to stand. She places a film holder behind his back then she and I step behind the glassed radiation shield. She yells out to Jake, "Can you hold your breath? I know it's painful."

"I think I can," he says.

"All right," the technician says, "on the count of three."

After the technician moves the machine several times for different views, the sonographer arrives with the ultrasound equipment. I watch him smear the jelly on the wand and gently move it over Jake's chest, and then I step outside and find myself engulfed in a commotion to rival a bee hive that's been hit with a stick. Jake's friend, Sam, practically bounces off the walls, as does the woman he's with, a statuesque brunette dressed in lime green and pink like she's in a time warp from the preppy handbook.

"I'm his fiancée," she screeches at the receptionist. "I demand to see him now. He needs me." Must be good old Claudia.

Sam pounds a fist in his hand. "Where's my buddy? Claudia heard a radio report about an accident on I-4, and when Jake didn't show up at the country club, she put two and two together."

I take over for the receptionist, who's looking a tad flustered by this larger-than-life duo. "Come with me, please." I motion for both of them to follow me. I wish I had a surgical mask to hide behind because I have an inkling Sam will be apoplectic when he gets a good look at me. I'll probably need to sedate him. I lead them into a very small visitors' lounge then I turn.

Sam checks my name tag then peers at my face. He jumps like he's on a pogo stick. "I'm in the freakin' Twilight Zone." He jerks a thumb at me and huffs. "Can we get a real doctor here?"

"What's wrong with you?" Claudia punches her brother in the arm. "She *is* a doctor." Claudia glares at me then she nods. "You know, you look familiar. I've seen your photo somewhere. Did you drop out of Junior League? You're not that provisional who got caught shoplifting, are you? I can't believe anyone would risk prosecution for a few bottles of nail polish. At least steal something valuable…like a diamond necklace."

Sam backs into a wall and points at me. "You stole someone's name tag."

In spite of my racing heart and a face that is surely red as a beet, I straighten my back and grapple for appropriate bedside manner. I need to be the calming presence here. I pull up a folding chair. "Please, have a seat before you fall down. Your friend is in shock and we don't need you to join him. We're doing X-rays and an ultrasound to determine the extent of his injuries. He may have some internal bleeding, but we'll know better once I get the reports back."

"When will that be, doctor?" Claudia asks. She's still looking at me like she's trying to figure something out.

Sam's mouth is moving like a guppy, but no words come out.

Claudia shakes her head at him. "What in the hell is wrong with you?"

I don't want to stick around to witness Sam's revelation to his sister…if he tells her.

I check my watch. "Those X-rays should be up. I'll have some news for you soon. In the meantime, I need to get back to the patient."

When I re-enter the X-ray room, the technician has posted the X-ray slides on the light box, as well as the ultrasound film. I study each of them carefully. "Good news," I say over my shoulder to

Jake. I breathe an internal sigh of gratitude. "You've got cracks in two anterior ribs, but they should knit back together quickly. No aortic injury or internal bleeding. With the kind of impact you sustained, you could have punctured a lung." Relief washes over me like a welcome breeze. "You're very lucky."

Jake stares at me. "I'll say. I didn't think I'd ever see you again."

My pulse quickens, but I choose to ignore his remark. "With rest, you should heal in three to six weeks. The bad news is that we don't cast broken ribs. The best we can do is bandage you or use a rib wrap, but that's up to you. It won't speed your healing, but it might protect the ribs from further injury. In the meantime, I'll remove the cervical collar now that I've seen the X-rays." I cradle his head. I want to run my fingers through his hair, but I snap myself back to the task at hand and busy myself with loosening the Velcro on the collar. I ease his head back on the pillow. "There, that should feel less confining." I pat his arm. His bicep flexes. Oh, my. "Coughing and laughing will hurt, and don't even think about taking a deep breath."

"Don't worry." Jake smiles. "I'm just happy to see you again."

I want to bend down and kiss him until my toes curl, which would be instantaneous, but I simply nod and smile. "Your friend, Sam, and your fiancée are here. Would you like to see them?"

Jakes' eyes grow wide. "Oh, God, did Sam see you?"

I nod. "He jumped so high, I thought his head was going to poke a hole in the ceiling. He doesn't believe I'm a doctor."

"Yeah, that would be our Sam." Jake coughs then winces. "I don't suppose I could have some pain medication? I'll probably need it before I face the twins."

"They're twins?"

"No, they're two years apart, but I call them the twins because they're so much alike."

Yikes, a female version of Sam? I pick up the chart that's attached to his gurney. "The EMT report says you're not allergic to any medications, correct?"

"No, not that I know of."

"Okay. I can get you something to make you more comfortable. We'll transfer you to a hospital room shortly."

"Can't I just go home?"

"I'd like to keep you overnight for observation. You've got some swelling around those ribs and I don't want any bones to shift and threaten a puncture. The less you move in the first twenty-four hours, the better." I walk out of his room. Thank God, he's going to be all right. On the way to the nurses' station, I wonder how many more times I'll get to see him before he's discharged. I can't help but smile, recalling our kiss over the ironing board. And here he is, flirting with me, but realistically, his behavior is due to shock. I'm the last person in the world he expected to see, so he let down his guard a bit.

He's engaged, Amy.

• • •

Jake

I squeeze my eyes shut and continue my shallow breathing. I'm almost panting, but if I take deeper breaths the pain is excruciating. They moved me to orthopedics on the fourth floor. I've got a lovely view of the parking deck.

Amy, or Dr. Maitland, said I'd heal in three to six weeks. Claudia will go ballistic if the wedding has to be delayed. But back to Dr. Maitland. Damn. When I saw her, I thought I'd died and gone to heaven. Without my glasses, she was blurry at first, but when I knew for sure it was her, I felt my heart would explode. Even in scrubs, she's adorable. I knew she was more than a fantasy maid, but a doctor? And she knows what she's doing. She's efficient and so caring. I'll bet she's great putting scared kids and nervous older folk at ease. The question is why is she working as a fantasy maid?

My musings are interrupted by the Three Stooges minus one when Sam and Claudia appear at my door. I reach for my glasses, then think better of it. The two of them in full focus can be sensory overload.

"Oh, my darling, what an adventure you've had!" Claudia races to my bedside and squeezes my arm, inadvertently bumping my side.

I see stars for a moment and puff shallow breaths until I recover. "I'll be fine. The doctor says I just need to rest for a few weeks."

"This better not delay our wedding." Claudia's eyebrows arch more than usual.

"Dr. Maitland says up to six weeks."

"Oh, surely we can fudge on that." She waves a hand in the air.

"We can strap him to a board," Sam says to his sister. "You know, carry him into the church and then prop him up." Sam chuckles.

"Really, Sam, this is no laughing matter. The love of my life is sprawled out like a beached porpoise here. If he's not in marching shape in two weeks, we'll simply have to come up with a Plan B." She taps a finger to her lips. "I'm wondering if a pair of Spanx would help?"

"That's the spirit, Sis." Sam finally turns his attention to me. "Listen, Buddy, I'm really sorry you're in this predicament, but hey, can you believe that doctor was your fantasy maid?" Sam slaps a hand over his mouth. Maybe he thinks I haven't recognized Amy.

I shoot a glance at Claudia. She's bobbing her head like she's been let in on the secret. Great.

"Um, yes, it was quite a surprise," I say.

"Surprise? I'd call it a shockeroo. Remember that movie, *Catch Me if You Can*? Leonardo was in a pickle when they thought he was a doctor. He didn't know a clamp from a scalpel." Sam shakes his head. "I'll bet she's just a good actress. She must have lied on her medical school application."

"Yeah, Sam filled me in. Talk about stranger than fiction. She probably puts out like a Pez dispenser," Claudia says. "She must be sleeping with the chief of staff."

"All right, that's enough," I say. I'm getting hot under the collar, even though I'm not wearing one. "She's legit. I'm sure of it. And she's a really good doctor."

Claudia purses her lips and her eyes get narrow. I know that expression. The cogs are turning.

"It's still pretty suspect, if you ask me." Sam rubs his chin. "Seems like something a serial killer would do. I read a book about this evil guy who masqueraded as a Park Avenue veterinarian. He was making money hand over fist."

"Oh, think of those poor poodles," Claudia says. "They're probably running around Manhattan rabid." She plucks a tissue from the box on my nightstand and dabs at her eyes…very carefully. Claudia would never be caught with smudged mascara.

That's when Dr. Maitland reappears.

• • •

Amy

"How's the patient?" I address Jake, but Claudia answers.

"He's better than good. I expect he'll be back to fabulous very soon." She winks at Jake.

"Perhaps not as soon as you'd like," I say. "Cracked ribs are near the top of the pain scale. They only heal with complete rest."

Claudia rolls her eyes. "You don't know my Jakey. He's bionic."

Jakey? "Given his excellent physical condition, I'm sure he's a good healer." Oh, I can't believe I said that. I can feel the blush creeping up my neck.

Claudia rounds on me. "What would you know about his physical condition?"

"She saw him naked in his apartment," Sam says.

"Not naked," Jake says. "I was wearing a towel."

"Oh, this is getting interesting." Claudia folds her arms across her chest and sways on her high heels. "I believe there's more to this fantasy maid tale than you fellows have shared with me." Her head bobs between Jake and Sam then she looks at me, pure venom in her eyes. "Are you some kind of pervert? Why would a doctor clean houses in a bikini?"

I want to slap her, but I grit my teeth and maintain my cool. "We're not here to discuss my...livelihood." I suppose that was a weird choice of words. Is my fantasy maid gig my livelihood? Oh, well, I forge on. "The patient needs to rest and you two should go. Visiting hours are over." I'm saved by the nurse, who appears at the door with a small tray and a big syringe. She walks to the bedside and checks Jake's wristband to verify his name.

"Egad," Claudia says. "That shot is monstrous. Sure it isn't for an elephant? I may faint dead away. You know how sympathetic I am." She fans herself with her hand.

"It goes in his IV, not his hip," I say.

"Thank goodness. You've already gotten an eyeful."

Now my ears are burning. I look straight at Jake. "Use that buzzer if you need anything during the night."

As I walk out the door, I hear Claudia say, "You better not buzz her for anything more than a shot."

• • •

Jake

"That was uncalled for, Claudia." I'm embarrassed for Amy, er, Dr. Maitland. "You were bitchy." The nurse injects the morphine into my IV. She barely leaves the room before a wave of sweet relief washes over me. But my sweet relief is short-lived.

"Bitchy? You haven't seen bitchy. I'll show you bitchy." Claudia huffs and heads for the door. Luckily, Sam grabs her arm before she can exit.

"Calm down, Sis. You've got nothing to worry about. Jake is squeaky clean. He didn't even want her to put on the bikini."

"Would you rather have her clean in the nude?" Claudia asks.

"No!" I practically yell, which hurts. I'm starting to feel woozy.

Claudia massages her temples. "Look, I'm sorry. You're the one in the hospital bed and I'm frazzled about how this might ruin my wedding day." She looks at Sam. "Big Brother and I will let you sleep. I'll be back in the morning and I promise to be in a better mood." She leans over and kisses me on the cheek.

Sam pats my arm and the siblings depart...finally. I've never seen Claudia so irrational. I don't like this new woman. It's as if she blames me for having an accident, which by the way, wasn't my fault. And her behavior toward Amy is inexcusable. Ah, Amy.

The drugs are kicking in big time now. Goodnight moon.

I dream I'm at the front of the church in my tux, stifling a sneeze. The sanctuary is covered in gardenias, my least favorite flower. I hate their cloying scent. I have a stabbing pain between the eyes. Sam is next to me. My dad and mom are in the front row and mom's crying. Maybe the gardenias have gotten to her, too. Dad keeps running his fingers under his collar. Is it hot in here? I wouldn't know. I'm numb.

The bridesmaids, in neon blue, take their places and we all look expectantly to the front of the church for the bride. Claudia wants to walk down the aisle to Pachelbel's Canon, so I'm surprised when Jason Mraz's "I'm Yours" begins to fill the church. I look at Sam, who just shrugs like it's the most natural thing in the world for his sister to change her mind at the last minute.

I flex my hands then fold them in front of me. I straighten, locking my knees. I start to teeter, but catch myself. I'm nauseated and there's no emesis pan in sight. The wedding guests along the aisle have all put on party hats and are blowing noisemakers…to the music. This I find a bit odd.

On her father's arm, Claudia glides toward the altar. From this distance, I can't see through her veil. Really, a veil? What is this, the 1950s? When her father hands her off to me, she raises the lace. It's not Claudia. It's Amy. And I'm thrilled, ecstatic, on the verge of hyperventilating. In fact, I'm so excited I can barely get through the ceremony. My cheeks hurt from grinning. I keep motioning for the minister to hurry things up. The more I motion, the slower he gets. When the pastor finally pronounces us man and wife, I kiss her quickly, pick her up, and literally run up the aisle. I carry her into a room off the antechamber. It's the room where the bride and her bridesmaids dress. I know this isn't proper. We must have a honeymoon planned, but I don't care. I have to have her this very moment.

She doesn't object to my urgency. In fact, she points to a settee and starts hiking up her floor length gown. She kneels on the settee. She's wearing a lace garter belt, shimmery nylons, and the sweetest little thong. Do women still wear garter belts? Amy does. I push aside her diminutive thong. I've waited my whole life for this moment, when I claim the woman I love as my own. My cock is the size of Mr. Green Jeans's prize cucumber. I slide into her and her sheath envelops me. She feels like crushed velvet, all soft and cushy, but at the same time, a perfect fit. She arches her back and grinds into me. I'm in to the hilt and I never want to leave. I'm so hot for her, I could come in a few thrusts, but I want her pleasure more than my own. I reach around her legs for her clitoris and begin a slow massage. She moans at my touch, throwing back her head. I thrust slowly and rhythmically as I circle her bud with my fingers. She pants, or is that me? She says, "Oh," and then "Oh, oh, oh," and then "Oh, oh, oh, oh." I grab her hips and pump as her climax comes in waves that caress my shaft and send me over the edge. She shudders violently and I immediately follow suit. I wrap my arms around her waist and hold fast to the woman I will love for the rest of my life.

Something nudges my shoulder.

"Wake up, Mr. Sinclair. I need to take your vitals."

I peel my eyelids open. A nurse is staring down at me and Amy stands in the doorway. Someone's made a tent in my bed. Oh, no, it's not a tent. It's my boner, sticking straight up like the main pole in a three-ring circus. Holy shit. It should be obvious that my vitals are, well, vital.

"You may be hurting, but you're still in working order." The nurse chuckles as she checks my wristband. She sticks a thermometer in my mouth and readies her blood pressure cuff.

Under the sheets, I push my boner down to half-mast as Amy approaches. She is so damn cute. I want her to straddle me.

She's smiling. "Are you able to sleep?"

"Uh, yeah." And dream.

"That's good." She picks up my wrist to take my pulse. Her hands are so beautiful and delicate. Uh, oh, here comes that boner again. Down boy!

"The EMTs filled in some of your medical history, but I'll need to verify a few things with you in the morning."

"Family history stuff?" I ask.

"Yes, mostly."

Suddenly I'm extremely curious about Amy's history. When the nurse walks out, I ask, "I know your grandfather owned a haberdashery, but what about the rest of your family?"

Her smile evaporates. "My dad was a pilot and my parents died in his small plane several years ago. A thunderstorm came up when he was over the Everglades so there was nowhere to land. He tried to ease it into a swamp, but a tree sheared off a wing." She sniffles. "It's still hard to talk about."

I want to wrap her in my arms, in spite of my cracked ribs. "I'm sure they'd be very proud of you."

"Well, I've wanted to be a doctor since I was a little girl, so they'd be proud I've realized that dream. Not so much for my other job, but it's been necessary."

"Is that why you've had to work as a fantasy maid, for the money?"

"What, you don't think cleaning houses in a bikini is a noble ambition?" The smile returns.

"Just seems a strange juxtaposition, considering you're a doctor."

"I'm a first year resident, or what they used to call an intern. Ellen and I are working under Dr. Adams in the ER. He typically would have been looking over my shoulder, but there were several accidents tonight, so that's why you haven't seen him. I've reported your condition to him and I'm sure he'll be in to see you soon. But to answer your question, I really can't make as much money doing anything else, especially considering the flexibility of the fantasy maid hours. I've got a small inheritance that covers my living expenses, but I've been pretty much on my own to pay for school." Amy stands next to my bed. I want her to touch me.

"Any brothers and sisters?"

"Would you believe five brothers?"

"They don't object to your other job?"

"They don't know. No one knows except my best friend, Ellen. And now you, Sam, and Claudia." She winces. Can't say I blame her.

"I don't want you working as a fantasy maid anymore." Not sure where I get off, telling her what to do, but it just came out.

She jams her hands on her hips and juts out her adorable little chin. "Pardon me, but what makes that any of your business?"

She could leave it at that. I feel duly chastised. But no, she has to rub it in.

"If there's one thing I can't tolerate, it's a man trying to tell me what I should do. I got it up to here," she does the chop motion at her neck, "when I was growing up with five brothers. They wanted to pay for medical school, but I knew they'd insist I go into sports medicine. Besides, I'd never hear the end of what they did for me." She shudders. "I am perfectly capable of making my own decisions about my life and you, Mr. Hot Shot, are not to pipe in with your two cents' worth." She pivots to leave. She doesn't look back. Over her shoulder she says, "I'll have someone else come in to take your family history."

Chapter Five

Amy

The seven A.M. shift is just changing as Ellen and I share coffee in the residents' lounge.

"It's not like you to overreact like that," she says, referencing my blowup with Jake, which I've just relayed. "You must really like this guy."

That perks me up. "Are you kidding? How arrogant could he be? He has no right telling me what to do with my life." No, but he could sure make some suggestions about my lower regions, as long as I get to tell him what to do with his at the same time. I stop myself from imagining the ways I want to ride him, taste him, put him inside me—the hard and fast ways I want him to ride me…Oh, cripes, I feel the heat rising in my cheeks.

"Maybe he's just concerned about you. You have to admit, there's potential danger every time you ring a new doorbell."

"Well, there's potential danger for the Avon lady, too."

Ellen laughs. "Come on, Amy, you can't compare someone who sells cosmetics fully clothed to a naked maid."

"I'm not completely naked."

Ellen throws up her hands. "Can you hear yourself? No, here's a better idea. Listen to Jake. If your brothers knew what you were doing, they'd lock you up."

"That's just it. I've spent my life trying to make my own way without the interference of my brothers. They've ruled my world since I was a kid. I couldn't even pick out my own Halloween costume. If they wanted a Star Wars theme, I had to be R2-D2. One year, they wanted to be cowboys."

"How bad could that be? You'd be a cute cowgirl."

"Oh, sure, that would have been fine. But I wasn't a cow*girl*, I was a *cow*." I huff, like a five-year-old. Oh, what the heck, I could use a good rant. "And I was always the one who had to ring the doorbell. Oh, sure, push the little girl to the front. She looks undernourished. Load her bag with candy. By the time we got home, my bag would be bursting. But did I get to keep the candy? Oh, no. The guys would dump it all out and then divvy it up. And while they were divvying, they'd be stuffing their faces. I'd be lucky to get an errant M&M."

Ellen laughs. "Okay, I get it. But this really isn't about your brothers, much as I wish it was." Ellen waggled her eyebrows like Groucho Marx, my mom's favorite comedian. I didn't know whether to laugh or cry. Evidently, the idea of my brothers got her hormones' attention. She shimmied, but there was no breast action to accompany her gyrating shoulders. Ellen looked down at her chest and shrugged. "I guess you need more than nipples to get the girls going."

"You don't know how lucky you are. I need a support bra to bake a cake." My thoughts stray to the ways Jake could help me with that issue: him naked behind me, his hands supporting my breasts while he whispers in my ear, telling me to concentrate on the cake instead of on his busy hands…I yank my unruly imagination back to the here and now—reluctantly, very reluctantly.

"Just once, I'd like to know how it feels to bounce." Ellen laughed. "But we're off point. Your brothers would strangle you if they found out about your maid job, but they're not the immediate threat."

"Tell me about it. If Jake's fiancée blows the whistle to the powers that be, it could ruin me."

"Okay, that's the conversation you should be having with Jake, making sure the witch keeps her trap shut." Ellen takes my hand. "But wait until I record his family history before you pass judgment."

"Thanks for taking that over, Ellen."

"Oh, hell, Amy, I'm just racking up Brownie points to get in good with your brothers." Ellen winks at me and sashays out of the residents' lounge.

• • •

Jake

I'm reading *TIME* magazine when I hear a gentle rap on my door. Laying the magazine on the bed, my heart thuds when I see a white lab coat, but when my eyes focus on the face, I realize my visitor isn't Dr. Maitland but another female resident. The woman snickers, possibly because my face falls? She extracts a pencil from her coat as she walks to my bed.

"Good afternoon, Mr. Sinclair, I'm Dr. Kurtz. I was with Dr. Maitland when you were admitted. I'm here to finish up your family history for our files."

"I'm afraid I scared Dr. Maitland off," I say.

"She doesn't scare so easily, but she was hopping mad."

"Yeah, she had a reason to be. I acted like a jerk."

"You just hit a nerve." Dr. Kurtz smiles. "Her brothers get under her skin."

Geez, I think, Amy must have shared our whole conversation.

Dr. Kurtz sits in the one bedside chair and flips open her file. She touches the lead pencil to her tongue and says, "Okay, I just have a few questions. First, are you a privileged, arrogant lawyer who's been handed the world on a silver platter?"

I can feel my features distorting in disbelief. I try to return to a neutral expression. I must not have heard her correctly. "What? That's not a standard medical history question—is it?"

45

She takes a deep breath, like she's getting ready for a lengthy interrogation. "It is when I'm holding the file. Amy's my best friend and I don't like to see her upset."

"Okay," I hear myself say, "Since I'd like nothing more than to be back in her good graces, I'll answer your 'standard' question. I wasn't a spoiled kid. I put myself through law school working as a waiter."

Dr. Kurtz nods and sits up a bit straighter in her chair. Her disapproval appears to be waning. "Tell me about your family."

"My parents were both schoolteachers. They're retired. They both love to fish and they raise bloodhounds. I have one sister who's a nurse. She lives in Ft. Lauderdale with her husband, who's also a nurse, and their three children." I pause. "You're not writing any of this down."

Dr. Kurtz taps the pencil to her temple. "I have a good memory." She gets up from her chair. "Any history of cancer, diabetes, or heart disease in the family?"

"My grandfather was diabetic."

"Any pulmonary disease, emphysema, nervous disorders?"

"No."

"Any surgeries?"

"I had a tonsillectomy when I was six."

"All right, Mr. Sinclair, everything seems to be in order." She walks to the door and turns. "Just a little advice to speed your recovery. Dump that smartass fiancée of yours and give Amy a shot."

I stare at the door after she leaves. I want to call her back, but what would I say? That Amy is the most perfect woman I ever met, but my timing sucks? I slam my fist on the mattress, which rattles the bed and sends a searing pain to my chest. I grit my teeth and squeeze my eyes shut. I breathe shallowly until the pain subsides and then I'm overcome with fatigue. Sleep, that's what I need.

A short while later I'm awakened by a new presence in my room.

"Excuse me, Mr. Sinclair?"

A tall, distinguished looking man in a crisp white lab coat is standing by my bedside. I must have been dozing. At least this time, I wasn't dreaming about Amy, so there's no boner to quell. I was in a jail cell. I don't want to theorize about the meaning of that. "Yes?"

"I'm Dr. Adams, the emergency physician supervising the residents. How are you feeling?" he asks as he reviews my chart.

"I've felt better," I say.

"I imagine so. You suffered quite a blow to your rib cage." He makes a note on the chart. "But everything seems to be in order with your care. I would have checked in earlier, but I believe you've been in good hands with Dr. Maitland?"

"The best," I say.

He meets my eyes. I'm sure I look like the first grader who's fallen in love with his teacher. "Yes, she's an excellent physician and very calm under pressure. I hope she'll consider emergency medicine as her specialty, though I believe she's leaning toward geriatrics."

"Really?" Now that I think about it, I can picture her with the elderly, soothing their woes with her calming presence and encouraging smile. She'd be the kind of doctor I'd want in my last days.

"Female doctors are frequently drawn to pediatrics, but it takes the same kind of care and understanding to deal with our older patients, many of whom are like children themselves," Dr. Adams says.

Just what I needed, another reason to admire her.

...

Amy

"Knock, knock." I'm at the door of Jake's hospital room. He's flat on his back, staring at the ceiling.

"I'd sit up to greet you, but I can't bend." He inclines his head my way.

"Yes, I know how it is with broken ribs. That's going to be your biggest challenge as you heal. You can get comfortable being prone and you're fine once you're upright, but getting there is a bear." I smile.

"Are you still mad at me?" His grin is sheepish…and sexy.

"Let's say you're reprieved." Here come those palpitations, dagnabbit.

"I'm glad."

We stare at each other. Moisture creeps under the arms of my scrubs. Oh, criminy, I'm fantasizing again. This time it's hospital bed sex wherein I test my abilities at keeping him prone and still while getting us both off. Hmm, if I straddle him and hover …

I shake my head—and my thoughts. "They're getting your paperwork together for discharge," I say. "Once you're out of here, you'll need to check back with an orthopedist in two weeks. I've included information about a couple of local clinics in your discharge packet." I avoid further eye contact in order to maintain a semblance of professionalism while everything south of my equator liquefies into a puddle of deep desire. And he hasn't even touched me.

"Thanks."

"And, um, I suppose this goes without saying, but I'd appreciate your discretion about the fantasy maid thing."

"I would never say anything to jeopardize your future, Dr. Maitland."

Oh, call me Amy, I think. The blatant and very carnal intimacy of my fantasies would certainly make first names appropriate. "Yes, I believe that, but some other people might not be as considerate."

"By other people, you mean Sam and Claudia."

"Precisely."

"I'll make sure their lips are sealed."

"Thanks." I steal a glance. My heart speeds up and my belly flutters. My imagination will not shut up: if you steal his hospital gown, he'll be naked—which is exactly where my next question will take us. "Well, would you like to get up and get dressed?"

"Absolutely. My undercarriage is numb."

We laugh.

He winces.

"I'll get a couple of aides to help. Be right back."

I fan my face as I move down the corridor. So maybe I can't control my visceral reactions, but at least I can be sensible. The man is not only engaged, he's my patient, and that makes him completely off limits!

* * *

Jake

Claudia and Sam, partially disguised by a huge vase of roses, stand in the doorway.

"Really, guys," I say, "you shouldn't have." Truly.

"Is my Jakey-poo ready to go home?"

The saccharin, little girl voice and the "Jakey-poo" grate like nails on chalkboard, but she thinks it's a term of endearment. She sets the roses on my nightstand. She picks up the small plastic emesis basin with two fingers and shoves it in the drawer. She can't help but say, "Yuck."

"The doctor is just getting some help to get me up, so yeah, I'm ready."

"Speaking of the doctor, I've just cooked her Cornish game hen." Claudia purses her pink lips, which match her Lacoste polo. The little embroidered alligator above her breast has never been more appropriate. I wish it would bite her.

Though I'm sure I know, I ask, "What do you mean?" I want to sic a bloodhound on her.

"Oh, I made a few targeted phone calls." She buffs her nails on her shirt.

I clench my fists. If I were standing, I'd punch a hole in the wall. "Claudia, how could you do that?" I try to prop myself on my elbows, but the pain is excruciating.

"Really, darling, do you think it's appropriate for a doctor to be wearing a bikini as her work attire?"

"It's none of your business, Claudia, and what she's doing is certainly not illegal." I inhale too deeply. Ouch.

"Oh, please, the reputation of this great institution is at stake."

My rage ramps up. My heart pounds and my chest throbs. Why am I engaged to her again? "Who did you tell?"

She looks at the ceiling, like she's trying to remember. She knows damn well who she called. "Let me see." She taps a finger to her nose. "Ah, yes, now I recall. I phoned the chief of staff here at the hospital and the chairman of the foundation board."

I want to throttle her. I ball my fists. I'd like to yell, but I can't suck in a big enough breath to pull it off. And then two orderlies enter my room, with Dr. Maitland right behind them.

"Oh, good, I'm glad you two are here," Dr. Maitland says to Claudia and Sam. "We can demonstrate how you'll need to help Mr. Sinclair get up and down." She nods to the orderlies, who take their places on either side of my bed.

"He can't bend in the middle, so the trick is to ease him off the side of the bed until his feet touch the floor. Make sure he doesn't hyper extend his back in the process then prop your hands behind him to keep his torso straight as you slowly lever him to a standing position."

The orderlies do as they're instructed and the discomfort is minimal. I'm far more upset with Claudia than with the pain in my ribs. I'm standing, though the room is spinning. Dr. Maitland reaches up and steadies me, both hands on my shoulders. I want to collapse in her arms and never leave. "Better sit down," she says. "It's natural for you to be light-headed after being on your back for so long."

Sweat tickles my brow. Amy reaches up to dab my forehead with a Kleenex, but then gives me the tissue. "We'll take you to your car in a wheelchair."

"I can walk."

"No, those are orders—and hospital policy. No slipping and falling on your way out." She smiles at me. She seems to be avoiding Claudia and Sam. Can't say I blame her there.

A nurse enters with a wheelchair. A plastic bag with my street clothes is in the seat; she hands the bag to Claudia, who holds it away from her like it's radioactive.

"Well, that should be it," Dr. Maitland says. "The aides will help you get dressed." She turns to Claudia and Sam. "I'm assuming you'll be his caregivers?"

They look at each other like who's on first. "Uh, yeah," Sam says.

"We'll be hiring a home health aide," Claudia says. "I really can't take the time away from my boutique." And then I suppose she feels compelled to add, "I just got in a new shipment of bikinis." She smirks at Dr. Maitland. "And of course, there's still so much to do to get ready for the wedding."

"Oh, that's right, I forgot about the big event." For a moment, Dr. Maitland's eyes meet mine. The corners of her mouth turn down then she recovers with a smile that's a bit too broad. "Best of luck," she says, "to all of you!" She backs out of the room. Her smile fades as she turns at the door.

• • •

Amy

I'm exhausted. ER duty is sleep deprivation on steroids. There are a few cots in the residents' lounge, but in addition to the discomfort of a canvas bed, there's too much commotion for me to catch more than a few moments of rest. All I want to do is head home. I retrieve my clothes from my locker, where a hospital green post-it greets me. "Call Dr. Reynolds," it says. My heart jolts. Jake promised he wouldn't say anything about my fantasy maid job, but why else would the chief of staff want to talk with me?

I wait until I get home to make the call. My hands are clammy as I punch in the number. I can't imagine that he'd be in his office, but horror of horrors, he is.

"Dr. Maitland?"

"Yes sir?" I bite my lip.

"I received a disturbing report today. While it has nothing to do with your exemplary academic record or your performance, it could reflect on the hospital."

Oh, criminy, here we go.

"I was told that you are working off hours as a maid who cleans in skimpy attire. Is that correct?"

Don't be defensive, Amy. Honesty is always the best policy. "Yes sir, it is."

"I have checked into this service. It appears to be legitimate, as much as something of such a prurient nature can be."

I cringe. Prurient?

"It would be beyond my jurisdiction to require you to quit this job, but I can see no reason why I shouldn't *suggest* that you terminate this extracurricular activity immediately."

I've got a lemon-sized lump in my throat, which I swallow with some difficulty. "Yes sir, I will—immediately."

"In that case, Dr. Maitland, I will forget I ever heard about this. Is that understood?"

"Yes, sir. Thank you." When I hang up the phone, I'm shaking. That could have gone much worse. I take a few deep breaths.

As my trembling subsides, another emotion kicks in. What happened to Jake's promise that he would make sure my job stayed under wraps? I remember the name of his law firm, Gray, Norton & Craig, from his medical chart, but of course, he won't be at work. I'm sure his cell or home number is on the chart. I call Ellen and ask her to get the number for me.

After I get home, I wait until dark to call Jake. I picture him flat on his back. As the phone rings, I hope he gets a major stab in his chest from reaching for it.

"Hello, this is Jake Sinclair." It's the greeting of someone who doesn't know who's calling.

"You couldn't leave it be, could you?" My voice cracks. I press a hand to my heart. I really liked him, drat the luck, or at least what I'd gotten to know about him during our brief acquaintance. More to the point, I'd really wanted to jump his bones, which is unforgiveable. Sure, I've been physically attracted to other guys, but Jake is special—or so I thought. I can't believe how disappointed I am in him for outing me. I'm mad, but I'm also deeply hurt.

"Amy?"

"Unless there's anyone else you've thrown off the bridge lately, yeah, it's me."

"I can't tell you how sorry I am about that." He sighs. I hope he had to take a deep breath and is now grimacing.

"You know, Mr. Sinclair, life doesn't always click along perfectly. Sometimes you have to scrape and scratch to get what you want. I'm not particularly proud of my work as a fantasy maid, but it pays my bills and I've done nothing to be ashamed of!" I realize my voice has risen at least an octave and that I'm shouting. Calm down, Amy.

"Have you quit your job?"

I stare at the phone. That was an interesting segue. "I'm going to quit. The chief of staff gave me an ultimatum of sorts."

He sighs again. "I truly am sorry about the hospital finding out, but I'm not sorry you won't be putting yourself in danger from potential whackos anymore."

"You don't get to feel sorry or not sorry, bucko. You just go and live your perfect little life with lovely Claudia. You deserve each other." I hang up. Tears well in my eyes and trace a hot path down my cheeks. I want to strangle Jake with gurney straps. I thought he was such a great guy. How could I have been so wrong?

Wait a minute, I tell myself as a thought strikes. He said he was sorry about the hospital finding out. That was an odd way to put it, like he might not have been the one to blab. Oh, what difference does it make? The damage has been done and there's no future with him anyway.

I try to conjure an unattractive image. Maybe he has out-of-control flatulence, or he picks his nose, or pulls his pants out of his butt. Maybe his feet smell. Somehow, none of those compute. Oh, well, onward and upward—or downward, as the case may be. Since I told Dr. Reynolds I'd give up being a fantasy maid in favor of my medical residency at Orlando Regional, I have to call Rex and tell him, too. Truth is I'm kind of relieved I have to quit being a fantasy maid. My residency schedule is a killer. I've already had to scale back significantly on my maid jobs, so maybe it won't be any more of a disappointment for him than it is to me.

Rex answers on the first ring. "Fantasy Maids, where your fondest dreams come with a Dustbuster." Rex thinks this is the height of great advertising.

"You might want to change Dustbuster to feather duster," I suggest. Not the first time I've suggested a switch in Rex's marketing.

"Oh, hi, hon. What's up?" He chews, loudly. I'm betting it's on a Philly cheese steak sub.

"I've got some bad news, Rex." I really hate to do this to him. He counts on me almost as much as I count on the cash to pay off my loans.

"Anybody hassling you? I'll tear them apart with my bare hands."

This would be amusing, as Rex is about five-foot-two and one hundred pounds. And that would only be if he was weighed immediately after consuming a Philly cheese steak.

"No, I have to quit, Rex."

There's a pregnant pause, then, "Seriously? You're my most reliable employee, not to mention the prettiest."

"I'm so sorry. I can't explain the reason, Rex. It's personal. If there was any way I could continue working for you, I would." I chew on my bottom lip.

"Do you need a loan? I know you're good for it. I wouldn't even charge interest."

"No, it's not a money issue." Well it is, but he's also been really good to me. "I won't leave you in the lurch. I want to be professional about this. How about two weeks' notice?"

Chewing ensues. A crunch signals the possibility he's bitten into a pepperoncini. "Actually, I need a little break," he says, sounding prosaic. "Three gals have quit recently, so I was just down to you and Rebecca. I don't think she'd mind a few weeks off. I think I'll head to Pennsylvania to see my mom and line up some new recruits."

"I appreciate your understanding, Rex."

"No problem, doll, but listen. I need you to do one last gig for me, okay?"

"Sure, I'd be happy to."

Rex gives me the address. As soon as we say our goodbyes, I phone Ellen.

"Kennedy Boulevard?" Her voice raises an octave. "That's a sketchy neighborhood, Amy. I can't believe Rex is sending you there."

"He's thorough about checking things out. I'm not worried."

"When is this job?"

"Next week. My last hurrah."

"Please don't put it like that. You know I get premonitions about things. Remember the time I stocked up on bottled water before I knew there was a hurricane on the way? This smells damn fishy to me."

•••

Jake

I welcome the pain of cracked ribs. When I focus on my chest imploding, it eases the emotional pain. A week ago, I was on top of the world. Now, everything I thought was good in my life has turned to shit. My fiancée has the compassion of a slug. I met a wonderful woman who thinks I'm an asshole and my best recourse is to leave it that way.

I can, however, cop an excuse for still being engaged to said callous slug. My pain meds have left me in such a fog, I'm unable to function much of the time. Otherwise, I'd surely have put an end to that personal misstep by now. I suppose I'm just delaying the inevitable. Besides, when I do call it quits with Claudia, I'll need to be well enough to duck. She'll surely fling any moveable objects at me, and I'll bet her aim is spot on.

Speaking of which, I hear my front door open.

"Darling, are you awake?" Claudia yells from the living room. "The brigade is here." She means Sam and herself. They're a brigade all right.

The two of them enter my bedroom like it's a combat zone. Their eyes dart from corner to corner.

"We're here to get you upright, buddy. The home health aide can't start until tomorrow." Sam laughs. "We could use a crane."

Claudia folds her arms across her chest. She squints.

"Aha, I've got it," she says. "Let's get the ironing board. We can ease him onto it then sort of cantilever him up."

"I don't think that's the right word, Claudia," Sam says. "It's more like a suspension." He rubs his chin.

I roll my eyes. "Engineering terms aside, let's try the ironing board."

Two minutes later, Claudia is bracing the ironing board and Sam has pushed me onto it. Actually, I'm half on the ironing board and half on the bed. My swat team stands back to assess the situation. As they rub their chins, I say, "Uh, I think I'm slipping."

"What we really need is a fork lift," Sam says.

I feel like a starfish splayed on a moving deck. The ironing board is creaking under me. My muscles tense.

"I believe I'll call the fire department," Claudia says.

Five minutes pass. I'm clutching the sides of the ironing board for dear life. The doorbell rings. Two burly guys with back supports securely fastened around their mid sections get on either side of me and hoist me up at the count of three.

"What were you trying to do here, bed surfing?" one of the firemen asks Claudia.

She bats her eyelashes at him. "Well, the poor fellow hasn't had much fun lately. We thought we'd liven things up." She backs up a foot or two so she can take in the breadth of this guy, who must be six-foot-five. The name "Maitland" is embroidered on his shirt. Oh, no, I'm hoping Claudia's near-sightedness will win and she won't see his name.

Too late.

"Maitland?" She asks. "You wouldn't by any chance have a relative who's a doctor, would you?"

"Yes, ma'am," he says. "My sister, Amy, is a doctor." He puffs out his formidable chest. I'd be proud of her, too, if I were him.

Claudia laughs. "Honey, she gets around. Just last week she was naked in my fiancé's apartment."

The guy looks at Claudia like she's got a screw loose, which she does. "You must be mistaken, ma'am."

"Oh, believe me, I'm not mistaken. You mean you didn't know what she did in her spare time?" Claudia puts 'spare time' in air quotes.

"Claudia, let it go." I try to maintain a smile, but with bared teeth, I doubt I'm successful.

Claudia smiles back at me like she's just won the lottery. "Why, darling, don't you think a brother has the right to know what his sister's up to? I certainly don't have any secrets from Sam." She punches Sam's arm and he nods like a robot.

I'm still propped between the firemen. "I'm steady now. You can let me go." I glance up at Fireman Maitland, whose slack jaw and wide eyes look like someone who's been thrown a grenade. He's just waiting for the explosion.

"Look, Claudia's been under quite a strain," I tell him while I glare at her. If she says one more word ...

"No problem," the other fireman says, looking at Claudia. "If you find yourself in the same situation tomorrow, call us before you try the ironing board." He looks Claudia up and down, and a smile blossoms. Maybe he'd like to come back to see her again.

Claudia's body undulates like a slow wave. She must be enjoying the attention. She reaches into the pocket of her Bermuda shorts and takes out a card. "We will definitely call again. If you're in the market for a nice trinket for your lady love, come visit me at my shop." She hands him her card and lets her hand slowly trail down his arm before stepping back.

The fireman gives Claudia a second once-over. "I don't have a lady love, but I might stop by…just to look."

Pain killers aside, am I a dolt or is my fiancée giving this guy the come-on right in front of me? Now that I'm upright I should probably just go ahead and offer them the bed. They're almost panting. I should be jealous, but I'm silently cheering them on. That's when my brain wakes from its medicated stupor, and I realize there's not a tinker's chance in hell I'll marry Claudia. I've let it go too close to our wedding date, but at least now I know what I need to do.

Meanwhile, Fireman Maitland doesn't say a word. I don't think he can speak. His shoulders slump. Poor guy.

His friend, on the other hand, is beaming like he's hit pay dirt.

When the firemen leave, Claudia and Sam dissolve in giggles. I suspect they're laughing over the further havoc they've wreaked in Dr. Amy Maitland's life, but the humor is lost on me. Of course, I've got more serious things on my mind, like rectifying the shambles of my life.

Sam checks his Rolex. "I've got to get to work. I'm in the running for top salesman this month. Need to rattle some chains." He waves his keys in front of my nose. He sells Porsches, or as he likes to call them, phallic symbols on wheels.

"Yeah, I need to go soon, too, darling," Claudia says. "Would you like me to plump your pillows?" She starts fluffing my pillows with gusto, like they're punching bags.

I walk Sam to the door then I turn to Claudia. "How about some coffee?"

"I'd rather have tea," Claudia says.

I head slowly to the kitchen and put the water on to boil. When Claudia enters, I motion for her to sit down. I don't sit. The only way I'm comfortable is either flat on my back or standing.

"This feels weird, me looking up at you." She chuckles. "I guess you won't have to sit down in the church."

"Claudia, there's no easy way to say this." I run a hand through my hair. "We need to cancel the wedding."

"We can't postpone," she whines. "Everything's booked."

"I didn't say postpone. I said cancel."

The tea kettle starts to whistle and Claudia rises from her chair. Steam from the kettle pales compared to the steam from her ears. "What the fuck are you trying to pull?"

I turn off the burner and let the whistling slowly subside. "See, there's the Claudia I didn't know existed until a few days ago."

"You mean back when I was sweet Claudia, game face Claudia? Listen, I can play demure with the best of them, but it's a tough world out there and you need someone who can stand up and fight." She punches a fist in the air, barely missing my chin. Maybe that's what she was aiming for.

"I'm not talking about spunk. I admire someone who can hold their own, but you're downright cruel."

"Because I tattled on that slutty doctor?" She slams her open palm on the kitchen counter. "Is that what this is about?"

"In a word, yes, because that's exactly what you did, tattled on her like an eight-year-old brat. And she's no slut. If it wasn't bad enough telling the chief of the hospital staff, you had to squeal to her brother!"

"You don't get to break up with me." Her eyes blaze.

"Fine. Tell everyone it was your decision."

"Oh, I will. I'll say you simply weren't worthy of me." She flips her hair and sticks her turned-up nose in the air. In a rain storm, she'd drown. "I hope your ribs stab you." She snatches her purse from the counter. The way she swings it around, I expect her to hit me with it. Just not on the ribs, please. She clutches it to her breast. Purple splotches bloom on her face. She's so mad she looks ready to burst a gasket.

Okay, I've faced angry juries. There's frequently a tipping point in the progression of a trial. Just when jurors are so caught up in the drama you think they'll never listen to reason, a simple thread of logic can put the issue in perspective and turn the course. I can certainly redirect this conversation. And I know Claudia's hot button, her ego. "In the long run—hell, even in the short run—I'd bore you, Claudia. You need someone more adventurous." I shrug. Ouch. "You're just too exciting for me."

"That's for damn sure. And by the way, those glasses I bought you really make you look nerdy." She bends down to adjust the strap on her designer shoe. I'm reminded of the statistic that forty percent of women have hurled footwear at a man. She seems to be contemplating it.

"You're like a firecracker and I'm nothing but fizzle." I mentally cross my fingers. I push my glasses up the bridge of my nose.

She huffs.

"You're a Mercedes and I'm an old, beat up jalopy." I sigh, resigned to my inferior plight.

She puffs out her chest and heads for the door, which she slams as she exits. I head to the window to make sure she doesn't deface any property on the way out, though she may dislocate her hips—they're swaying from here to Daytona Beach. She's probably envisioning her next conquest. Thank God, I dodged the bullet.

I realize I've been wearing my shoulders under my ears, which hasn't helped my ribs. I roll my neck and take a few cleansing breaths, not too deep.

Ironic how I wouldn't have recognized Claudia's vindictive streak if I hadn't met Amy.

Amy. Well, I messed that up royally. She thinks I blew the whistle on her. I've missed my chance with the most wonderful woman I've ever met.

Most of the time I'm a positive guy; when life gets me down, I've always been able to pull myself out of my doldrums. Right now, though, all I want to do is find a black hole and dive in.

Chapter Six

Amy

"I can't believe you roped me into a blind date." Though it feels like years, it's only been a few days since the fiasco with Jake Sinclair and the big rat out to the chief of staff. Ellen and I are walking into Hue Bar, one of the trendiest hangouts for singles in Orlando. I set her up with Matt, but she insisted we double-date, so Matt is bringing one of his co-firemen for me.

"Come on, who can resist a hunky fireman?" Ellen's on tiptoes, which in stilettos is quite the feat, surveying the guys at the bar. "There's Matt," she says…with a shimmy. Why is it I already feel like a third wheel?

I look beyond Matt to his buddy. We lock eyes. I gulp. Between this guy and my brother, next year's hunky firemen calendar is well on its way to publication. He's broad as a tank and his eyes are amber. I'm reminded of the vampires in the Twilight saga. Perhaps this guy thirsts for blood, too.

"Hey, Sis." Matt hops off the barstool and grabs my arm. Yeow. I'll surely have a bruise.

"Hey, Bruto." I kiss him on the cheek. All my brothers have nicknames. Matt became Bruto for his girth. Though he could have just as easily been Dopey.

"This here's Aaron." Matt gesture with his thumb to the hunk sitting next to him. "Hey, that's two 'A' names. Amy and Aaron, sitting in a tree, k-i-s-s-i-n-g."

"Don't get ahead of yourself." I try to pinch my brother on his washboard abs, but I can't get enough skin. I look at Ellen, who's licking her lips.

"I think you two already know each other." I look back and forth between Matt and Ellen. They must have heard me, but you'd never know it from the vapid expression on both their faces. They're already entranced.

Matt offers Ellen his barstool.

She slides onto it. In fact, she has to grip the bar so she doesn't slide off. Cotton on fake leather has that effect. Frankly, her miniskirt's so short I'm surprised her thighs don't stick to the barstool like adhesive. She adjusts her bum and bats her eyes at Matt.

"We met at the graduation," Ellen says, proffering her hand in that limp kind of way that says, *'Save me, I'm helpless'.*

I just hope she doesn't give Matt the wrong impression. He's a face value kind of guy. If Ellen acts like she needs a protector, he'll be right there. And Ellen needs almost as much protecting as a Tasmanian devil.

I look back at Matt, who's frowning at me. "The weirdest thing happened yesterday." He scrubs his hand over his chin. "Aaron and me were at this apartment helping a guy with broken ribs get out of bed and the woman who called us tells me something about you being naked in this guy's apartment."

Good old subtle Matt. He couldn't have pulled me aside? My heart starts beating in my ears.

"Oh, that." I shoot Ellen a look. Her eyes are as big as silver dollars. "That was a masquerade thing that the, uh, hospital was doing to raise money for, uh, the new orthopedic wing." I smile innocently. "And I wasn't naked. I had on a bikini."

"Wish I'd been there," Aaron says.

Matt squints and purses his lips, standard procedure for mulling things over. He nods then shrugs. "Okay." Slapping his thighs, he says, "What do you beautiful ladies want to drink?"

I can't tell you the times I've counted my blessings for having a gullible brother. I almost feel bad for lying to him, but it's always been just too easy. There's not a conspiratorial bone in his body and he always sees the best in everyone. I give him a big hug.

"What was that for?" he asks when I finally let him go.

"That was just for being you." I look at Ellen, who swipes a finger, *whew*, across her forehead. "If I know Ellen, she'll want the same thing I'm having, nonalcoholic beer." I inhale the smoky aroma of aged scotch that wafts from behind the bar. I'd love one, but Ellen and I are on call.

Ellen nods and takes me by the elbow. "Will you two excuse us while we go powder our noses?"

"Your noses look fine to me," Matt says.

Ellen smiles demurely. "You men have it so easy. You just throw on some clothes and go. We women have to work so much harder at looking good." She bats her eyelashes. This is so not Ellen.

We turn for the bathroom. I'm making a beeline, but Ellen pulls me back. She whispers in my ear, "Slow down. Let them get a look at the rear view."

"What has gotten into you?" I ask as I pull open the bathroom door. "Who kidnapped my best friend?"

She slaps my arm then goes dreamy-eyed. "Your brother makes me want to be barefoot and pregnant for the rest of my life."

I take her chin in my hand, which isn't easy since she's about a foot taller than me. "Listen to me carefully. You're a brilliant woman and Matt's, well, far from it. He's sweet and gorgeous, but you're never going to have an intellectual conversation with him."

Ellen looks down at me with warmth in her eyes. "Honey, I'll take emotional intelligence over intellect any day. I've had brilliant boyfriends who were as empathetic as a doorknob. I'm going for cozy and sexy." She smiles. "And Aaron looks like he could supply that, too, if you're in the market."

"I found my perfect man, but unfortunately, he's someone else's." I move to the bathroom mirror, where I pout at myself.

"Hang it up, Amy. He's engaged to the wicked witch of the north. If he's crazy enough to marry her, they'll be the match made in hell. And besides, a bird in the hand…" She looks sideways at me and winks. "Well, you know what they say about pocketing a hot cock…"

She laughs and then turns to slather on her lip gloss and chuck it back in her purse. However, ah, *pointed* the suggestion regarding Aaron's assets, she's right about Jake. He's out of the picture, and a little recreational slap and tickle with Aaron might be just the thing to resurrect my spirits.

I take a deep breath and do my own slathering. Hmm, strawberry flavored. Not bad.

She nods at me in the mirror. "Let's go."

I'm really not into this, but hey, it's just one night. I smile at Ellen and motion for her to lead the way. As I walk behind her, watching her hips sway, I wish I were anywhere else, like at home in bed…alone…or panting hot and heavy under the covers while Jake tongues my clit and makes me crazy until I come. Oh, criminy. I blink. I'm squishy *down there* at the mere idea of it.

By the time we get back to the bar, my sex is clenching and my head is spinning. To make matters even more uncomfortable, Aaron's off his barstool in one fluid motion and before I can protest, he lifts me by the waist to sit me down where he's been. My beer, in a frosty glass, invites a sip. I take one, hoping it will cool me down, but not realizing how thirsty I am. When I take a much bigger gulp, I can feel the foam mustache on my upper lip as I emerge from the glass. But I don't get the chance to lick it off because Aaron swipes his thumb across my lip, and then he licks the foam off his thumb, looking straight into my eyes while he does it. My nipples suddenly go hard and strain against my bra. My belly tightens with the wild notion that I wrap my tongue around his thumb and suck until both of us start smoking from all orifices. Did anyone else see sparks fly? I sure felt them.

"I've never been out with a doctor before," he says, his eyes smiling.

"Don't think of her as a doctor," Matt interjects. "She's just my bratty little sister." He pinches me. Ouch.

"Or," Ellen says, batting her eyelashes at Matt, "think of us as the most desirable women you've ever met."

I can't believe she said that. Matt's so open to suggestion, there's no telling what thoughts are coursing through his thick head.

"I don't know, I've always had a thing for women in scrubs," Aaron says. "It's not a negative in my book." He gives me the slow once over, and my scalp prickles.

I take another swig of my beer and while Aaron looks at Matt, I sneak a quick top-to-bottom. His hair is cropped very short, possibly to disguise a receding hairline. On him, it's sexy. I suppose you have to have a nicely-shaped head to pull off bald or close to it and his is cue ball perfect. His eyes are amber, did I mention that? Now that he's closer, I can see flecks of brown in them. I guess they're more caramel than amber. Mesmerizing is what they are. Full lips, a strong chin, and thick neck (he probably played football in high school/college), which I find attractive in a caveman sort of way. Egad, I'm starting to sound like Ellen. He's wearing a plain black t-shirt and of course his biceps and shoulders are to die for. Stonewashed jeans belted by Harley Davidson (wouldn't you know?) pool lazily over Frye boots. Very nice. When my eyes travel back up his torso, he's looking at me, no doubt realizing I've just made an assessment.

"So, what do you think?" he asks.

I clunk my beer glass on my tooth. Ouch. I have to run my tongue across my front teeth, but it's really a diversionary tactic.

He's hot, and I'm starting to way overheat in places I'd had no intention of using when I agreed to this double blind date. I need a moment to compose my answer. "I think you could have any woman in this bar and probably any woman in Orlando." Was that a considered response? No.

Aaron rears his head back and laughs. It's a low, guttural sound. Sexy. When he looks back at me, his pupils are dilated; I don't think it's because of the dark bar. "I appreciate your review, but I'm not interested in women who take me at face value. I want someone who can peel away the layers."

Wow, I think, maybe this guy has a brain. Meaning that aside from his physical girth and overall sex appeal, he's nothing like my brother. Matt has no layers. He wouldn't know a layer if it bit him in the butt. I'm not saying Matt's shallow because he's extremely generous and kind-hearted, but he never digs below the surface to look at motivation or how one's words might not mirror one's actions. He's a face value kind of guy, which is really pretty cool. God knows, he's a happier camper than most of us, but if you're looking for a philosophical conversation, Matt's not your guy. I wonder if he'll be enough for Ellen, though as I see the adoring way she's looking at him, maybe he will. History has surely witnessed stranger romantic entanglements.

Okay, back to the gorgeous man who has propped one hand next to mine on the bar. He smells like leather. I inhale deeply. "How many layers before a woman reaches your core?"

His eyes grow wide. I think he liked the question.

"Ever suck on one of those monstrous jaw breakers?" he asks.

I nod, and my imagination starts to rock with images of monstrous things a person might suck on. Cripes, this is so not like me! I must really need a distraction, and I have to admit I'm intrigued. Where's he going with this?

"I was a poor kid, so I'd make my jaw breakers last a long time. I used to play a game of counting the layers and I'd only allow myself one layer a day. There was a lot of finesse involved. If I didn't lick precisely, I'd end up with a dull brown, the result of a blending of two colors. But if I licked too much, I'd obliterate an entire color. I wouldn't remember all the colors I went through to reach the core, but I always remembered the last color."

Now that was a good speech. I think he had me at the poor kid statement. He's probably used this story a million times with other women, but for tonight, I'll pretend I'm the only one. "Which was?"

"Purple, always purple." He smiles.

"Ah, the color of good judgment."

"Also the color of romance and passion."

Maybe it's my disappointment over Jake, but I feel myself leaning into Aaron. My body is definitely in need, and while my conscience is telling me to pull away, my juices are pushing me over the edge. Aaron's pupils are almost black as he closes in and plants a soft kiss on my lips. I melt into him, and he steps between my knees and lifts me off the barstool. The temperature between us is volcanic when he grips my bottom and folds me in his strong arms. Do I care we're in a public place? Not for a nanosecond.

A punch in the ribs brings me back to earth. "We're heading out for a bite to eat. Want to join us?" The guys probably didn't notice, but Ellen gave me an almost imperceptible head shake as she asks this. She wants the two of us to head out separately with our respective dates. Aha.

My suddenly irrepressible libido dances a jig that some distant part of me is fairly certain I should be ashamed of.

"No, you guys go on." I smile at Ellen, who's never looked happier. Her returning smile shows both her teeth and her gums, it's that broad. "Oh, wait, you drove."

"I'll take you home," Aaron says.

I'm still pressed up against him when I notice, yep, that long, thick rod against my stomach is a sure indication of just how glad he'd be to take me home...and then some.

"Fine, but you'll need to feed me first." My tummy is rumbling. I'm surprised he can't feel it against his erection.

"Happy to, you like barbeque?"

"Love it." Truly I do.

"Let's walk across the street to Wildfire's. They serve a mean barbeque and great coleslaw, too."

We bid Ellen and Matt goodnight. Ellen fairly floats out of Hue and Matt seems pleased as punch himself as he slaps a big tip on the bar—my brother, the big spender. Actually, he's not trying to impress Ellen. He's just generous.

Aaron and I walk to Wildfire's. He takes my hand as we cross the street. Very nice.

The waiter knows Aaron and seats us on the patio under a string of twinkly lights. I notice the waitresses skittering around and whispering. They know Aaron, too. He shoots them a quick salute. He's probably slept with all of them. I find myself wanting to join the ranks of Aaron's groupies.

I order another nonalcoholic beer and Aaron gets a Corona. He sucks on his lime, which I find inordinately sexy then he stuffs it down his longneck bottle before taking a long draw.

"Something I need to know," Aaron says. "I was with Matt when we rescued that fellow with the cracked ribs."

Oh, no. I try to keep my face neutral. I blow my bangs out of my eyes, which might have worked if my bangs were in my eyes. As it is, it just looks like I'm blowing air up my nose. Guilty.

Aaron laughs. "I don't know what that woman had against you, but she seemed mighty excited to give your brother her news."

"She already got me in a heap of trouble, but I guess she couldn't leave it at that. Thank God I was able to redirect Matt."

"Your brother's the nicest guy I know. He'll always believe the best, particularly when it's someone he cares about." Aaron's eyebrows go up. I take it as a sign he wants the rest of the story. He's not getting it.

"Look, it's a moot point, now. She mistook me for someone I'm not, and that's the end of it. Fortunately, I landed on my feet."

Aaron salutes me with his bottle. "Like a cat."

No, not exactly like a cat. I'm not the sneaky type. But I'll let Aaron think I'm a cat. Someone he wants to pet and rub up against, except...

The mention of Claudia has broken the spell this handsome man had me under.

I just want to go home—alone—where I can nurse my wounds and eventually get over them. I've been downright coquettish tonight, and while I was caught up in this dynamic man's vibe, it's all a ruse. I'm no party girl.

When our barbeque arrives, we both eat heartily. I'm glad for the interruption in our conversation. This fellow is a player and I'm not into players—never have been. I suppose there's something flattering about being with a man who turns heads, but the real appeal for me is a fellow who doesn't notice the effect he has on women...like Jake. Aaron, on the other hand, is well aware of his magnetism. And ultimately, he's not the kind of guy I want for the long haul. I look him over somewhat regretfully and am reminded of a line from Shakespeare—"to thine own self be true."

Chapter Seven

Amy

The next day, Ellen grabs my arm and pulls me into the supply closet. "How'd it go with Aaron?" Her eyebrows wag.

I sigh. "It was fine. He's very nice, but I think the stress of the last few days finally got to me. I wasn't into a romantic evening." I grimace when she looks surprised, knowing further explanation is necessary after I let Aaron hoist me onto the barstool while we stuck our tongues down each other's throats. "I suppose I wanted to be with him, but then he brought up the incident at Jake's apartment where lovely Claudia spilled the beans to Matt and..." I shrug and Ellen picks up my train of thought.

"...and things fizzled when you let your head get in the way of simply enjoying yourself for a change."

I wince. She's not wrong, but I wish...well, I wish I could erase the Jake-and-Claudia episode and my brain lapse over a guy I have no future with. "I guess," I say.

Ellen pats my arm. "It's okay. I got romantic enough for both of us." Her eyebrows disappear into her bangs.

"With these eighty hour weeks we're pulling, I'm amazed you had the energy. I'll admit that Aaron was enticing, but I got to the point that I could barely keep my eyes open." I'm lying and she knows it.

"Uhn uhn." She shakes her head. I hate it when she sees through me. "You had plenty of energy. Your problem is that you're still hung up on Jake."

The mention of his name makes my knees tremble. "I don't want to be. Maybe it's just that he's unavailable and that makes him enticing." I shrug.

"Nah, he was a keeper, but I bet if you gave Aaron a chance, he could get Jake out of your head."

"Well, my next night off from the hospital, I'm working. It's my last maid's job. There won't be another chance until next month."

"Oh, good grief, I almost forgot about that. It's coming right up, isn't it?" Ellen chews on her lip.

"Stop looking so worried."

Ellen pats my arm again. "You know I'm very nervous about this location Rex is sending you to."

Truth be known, I am, too, but Rex has always been adamant about keeping his girls safe. I can't let him down. "Ellen, I'll be fine."

She adjusts her scrubs like they're chafing, which would never happen because they're roomy enough for a gorilla. "I suppose I can't talk you out of it, so..." She smiles. "Are you ready to hear about your brother and me?"

I really don't want to hear about my brother's sexual exploits, but I did set them up, and she is my best friend. So, I guess I have no choice. "I've got five minutes. Should I sit down?"

"Yeah, you'd better." Ellen takes a big breath.

I pull a folding chair from the wall and sit. "I'm ready."

"I think I'm in love." She flaps her hands in the air and almost levitates.

I've known Ellen for five years, but this is the first time I've seen her smitten, so I know to take this seriously. "Honestly, you couldn't have chosen a nicer guy." I smile.

"I know." She grins.

I'm more than a little amazed that this brilliant woman has fallen for my slow brother at all, never mind so quickly, but then again who can account for love? Matt is the kindest soul and by

God, that's what really matters. "With our wacky schedule, when are you going to see him, again?"

"I don't have another night off until week after next, but Matt said he's going to try to meet me in the hospital cafeteria for meals whenever he can."

That is so sweet and so like Matt. I'm smiling to myself when the door swings open and there stands the big fireman himself… with a sheepish grin on his face.

"You gals, oh excuse me, you doctors got time for a cup of coffee?"

"No, not even close," I say. I probably should have deferred to Ellen. I slap a hand over my mouth then regroup. "Uh, at least I don't." That's when I see Aaron standing behind Matt. My ears get hot. I have no clue what that means. All I can manage to say is, "Hi."

"Hope you don't mind that I tagged along," Aaron says.

Mind? Except that I'm kind of embarrassed by the way I led him on at the bar when I know I don't want to get involved with him. Why would I mind? "No, I'm just swamped. Gotta go." I squeeze past Matt and pick up my pace down the hospital corridor. I'm not quick enough for Aaron, though. He's right beside me.

"Listen," he says while we're both still in motion, my steps two to every one of his, "the last thing you probably want is a man in your life, but I'd really like to get to know you better."

I stop. I look up and down the corridor, where heads have popped out of rooms. Those would be radiology technicians and certified nursing assistants, all female, who are craning to get a look at the gorgeous fireman. Did I mention he's calendar worthy? "Aaron, right now is not the best time for me. Besides working eighty hour weeks, I'm just wrapping up a part time job."

"The naked thing?" He has the good sense to stage whisper. "I'm still mighty curious about that."

"Believe me, it's not something to worry your pretty little head about." I can't believe I said that.

He laughs. "Just trying to peel away a layer or two."

Really, I don't need one more person knowing about my fantasy maid job, especially someone who's so close to one of my brothers. Except for Ellen, I'd managed to keep my job under wraps for two years, even though I'd had more than a few close calls with the siblings. Now it seemed like the world was poised for a big announcement.

"Look," I say, "I think you're …" what, smart, gorgeous, intriguing, hot? Snap assessment to him being a player aside, I don't really know him so there's not much I can say about his character at this point. "I think you're interesting, but I'm not in a position to get involved right now." Besides which, I'm still carrying a tiny—okay, I'm lying to myself, a *huge*—torch for Mr. Unavailable.

He throws up his hands and begins to back down the corridor. "All right, Babe, your call. I was hoping for a peek under those scrubs." This time, his voice is louder than a stage whisper. Maybe he wants the hospital staff to hear him? Maybe my snap assessment of him was right after all. Except he's more than a player: he's Claudia wrapped up in an XY chromosome. I need to get as far away from him as possible—and stay there.

I start to say that I need to get back to work, but I don't even want to grant him that much response. I turn on my heel and head to the nurses' station.

Aaron calls after me, "I guess I'll have to give Claudia a call."

That stops me in my tracks. Did he really say that? I turn and walk back to him. I gather up my five-foot-three to about five-foot-three-and-a-half, take a deep breath, and say, "That's an excellent idea. I think you'll find her much more your speed." I stand my ground. It's his turn to walk away, which he does with a wave over his shoulder.

Oh, great, now all I have to do is wait for the perfect storm of the five Maitland brothers pouncing on me after Claudia gives Aaron the lurid details of my moonlighting job. A chill up my spine throws me into a full body jerk, and I rub my arms to recover. I need to stop being afraid of my brothers' opinions of me. I'm no longer the little girl they felt obligated to raise. I'm a medical doctor, for Pete's sake. I'm responsible for other people's lives, so I can surely take care of myself. God, I can't think about this now. I have patients to consider. How many hours are left in this shift?

What seems like an eternity eventually morphs into seven A.M., and my shift is finally over. I'm bone tired, but I need to talk to Ellen before we both head home for some shut eye. I catch her in the residents' lounge. She's in the midst of an enormous yawn.

"Before you leave, I need a big favor." I bounce on my toes. Where did this energy come from? Guess I'm a bit anxious.

"As long as I don't have to do anything until after my nap..." She tilts her head to one side and squints.

"Absolutely. Go home and collapse then ask Matt to come over."

"That's a no-brainer." Her slow smile builds.

"Calm down. I'm going to be there, too."

"So spill." She tugs on the sleeve of my scrub.

"I don't think Aaron's such a fine, upstanding guy. He said he's going to get in touch with Claudia so he can get to the bottom of the naked comment she made about me being in Jake's apartment. I'm sure she'll be only too happy to elaborate on my job."

"Oh, no. And then Aaron will tell Matt."

"Exactly. He's Claudia with a cock. He didn't take well to me rejecting him, so his way of getting back at me will be spilling the beans to Matt."

"So you want to soften the blow."

I nod slowly. "I never dreamed it would escalate to this, but there's actually something strangely comforting about having one of my brothers know the truth. And of all of them, Matt's the most understanding. I'm hoping that you and I can bring him around and also swear him to secrecy."

"I'll see if I can get him to come over at five-thirty. Do you think we'll need more than half an hour?"

"Oh, God, no. That should give him time for a few questions. And anyway, he'd nod off at a lengthy explanation. We just need to be persuasive."

"Okay. Unless you hear otherwise, I'll see you at my apartment."

I rub the back of my neck, where my muscles have tensed and a headache is creeping in. "Matt's always thought I was beyond reproach. This could really shock him."

"Go home and sleep on it. We'll make him see the light."

"I admire your confidence, because if Matt runs to our brothers, they'll weld me into a chastity belt." I picture myself clanking down the hospital corridor, a chastity belt securely fastened under my scrubs. Oh, cripes.

Chapter Eight

Jake

Claudia's Chanel hangs in the air like Los Angeles smog. I wonder what would counteract it. Roach spray? All I know is that I want any vestiges of her gone from my life and that includes everything from her lingerie in my dresser to her organic tea in my kitchen cabinet.

I start gathering up her stuff and putting it in a box. As I open a low drawer, I have to remember to bend at the knees and not at the waist. Ouch.

My doorbell chimes. It's probably a runner from the firm, delivering some work I requested. I'll be glad when I can get back to my office, but for now, I can't drive and I haven't worn a suit since they cut the one off me after the accident. My five o'clock shadow is three days old. I look like a guy who rifled through the Goodwill box and came up with mismatched sweats.

I peek through the peep hole in my door. It's not the runner from my office. It's Sam. Given he introduced me to Claudia and helped her make Amy's life miserable, he's not who I want to see. He'll probably offer to give me a shave then inadvertently slice my neck. I take a deep breath then open the door.

"You still pissed?" Sam fidgets with his car keys.

"My quarrel's not with you, Sam, and honestly, it's not about being pissed. It's about being disappointed in someone I thought I knew." Actually, there'd be no sense being disappointed in Sam.

He's the same guy he's always been, and I knew the kind of chaos he enjoyed going in. I step aside to let him enter.

"Yeah, Claudia was pissed enough for an army, but she's calmed down."

"Really?" I feel my eyes narrow. Knowing what I do about her now, Claudia calming down could be good for everyone…or very, very bad. "I'm surprised to hear that."

"Oh, I'm not saying she wouldn't do something vindictive if it fell in her lap, but I don't think she's wasting time on how she could fry your ass."

I grimace. "And I thought you knew her."

Sam chuckles. "Yeah, she probably would be scheming, but something else is distracting her. That's what I came to tell you. I thought you'd get a kick out of knowing that one of the firemen who got you out of bed showed up at Claudia's store this afternoon. When I popped in to see how she was doing, they were getting it on in the alley behind the store." Sam pockets his keys and sticks both thumbs up.

My mind races ahead in an attempt to assess possible collateral damage. Maybe Claudia's taking a contract out on me and is hiring this guy for the dastardly deed. And then it hits me. "Which fireman was it?"

"It wasn't the doc's brother, if that's what you're asking." Sam laughs. "This guy and Claudia were making eyes at each other when they got you out of bed, so it doesn't shock me."

"Face it, nothing shocks you, Sam." I clip him on the shoulder. "But I'm shocked you're still talking to me."

"Oh, shit, think I don't know Claudia? I always wondered how long it would take for you to see her true colors. She's my sister and I love her, but she's been a terror since she was two. That was the year she set the cat on fire." Sam shrugs. When he continues, he avoids eye contact. "Your life would have been a living hell."

So why didn't he try to enlighten me earlier? I should probably be relieved he's told me now, but I have an empty feeling in the pit of my stomach. Something doesn't add up. Claudia might be temporarily distracted from hammering me, but this fireman works with Amy's brother. Would Claudia still want to destroy Amy's reputation?

"What's up, man?" Sam asks. "You look like you're grinding your teeth."

I will my body to relax. I can't tell him what I'm thinking because, when all's said and done, I don't trust him. I wonder if I ever did. "Nothing." I rub my forehead. "I'm glad you came by. I'm just boxing up Claudia's stuff. Would you mind taking it to her?"

"Sure. The way she was going at it with that fireman, maybe I should just take the stuff to his place."

I hand him the box. "To the victor belong the spoils."

"I guess that's one way to look at it." Sam shrugs.

I open the door for him and after I close it, I breathe a sigh of relief...but not too deep. I'm glad to be rid of Claudia, no remorse there. If she takes up with this fireman, maybe she'll forget about Amy. Or, she'll enlist the fireman to help her get at Amy. I wouldn't put it past her. I don't care what lies Claudia spreads about me, but if she aims her claws at Amy ...

Ah, hell. Why would I have the right to do anything, the way I behaved? I could have raked Claudia over the coals when she called the hospital administrator, or even called him myself to tell him, what, that Amy Maitland is a wonderful doctor and a fine human being? I'm sure he knows that. Anyone who met her would know that. I clench my fists; my breaths come short and rapid. I order myself to calm down. Surely, Claudia will move on. Surely.

• • •

Amy

Arriving at Ellen's, I see that despite my intention to get to her house before Matt, I've failed. I should have known my brother would be early, not only because he's always early, but because he wants to spend as much time as he can with Ellen. I don't know what pretense Ellen used to invite him over this afternoon—or even if she had to use any now that they seem to be an item. Still, she may have said we wanted to talk to him about something serious, but that wouldn't pique Matt's curiosity. As I've mentioned, he deals in the here and now, not what might be or has been.

I sigh deeply and get out of my car. Ordinarily, I'd walk into Ellen's house without knocking, but today I rap on the front door. Don't want to interrupt a scene of carnal lust, especially not one involving my brothers. That's an image I do *not* want burned into my eyeballs for all time. I make a mock-gag face at the thought, and then chuckle to myself, enjoying a moment of levity before the shit hits the fan.

Ellen opens the door. She's flushed. Glad I knocked.

"Hi," she says, dipping her head. "Come on in. Matt and I were just…"

"Uh-huh." I smile and squeeze Ellen's arm. I am so happy for her. Matt's sitting on the sofa. He would typically rise to greet me, but he probably can't get up without revealing the rise in his pants. I sit on the other end of the couch and fold my hands in my lap. I shoot a look at Ellen, who pulls up a chair to the middle of the couch so that we're sitting in a sort of triangle.

Ellen looks at Matt. "You're probably wondering why we called this meeting," she says.

"Not really." There's no guile in his smile. Maybe he's forgotten he's here for something more than to see her.

Ellen slaps her thighs. "Well, Amy and I need to let you in on something that we've kept a secret just between us for a couple of years, but now we think it's time for you to know about it, too." She nods at me. I like the inclusive way she's setting this up.

Matt sits a bit taller. He's paying attention.

Ellen looks at me. She crosses her legs and jitters one foot. I nod to her. She takes a deep breath. "Okay, Matt, it's like this. Amy here," she sweeps her hand at me, like he needs to know who she's referring to, "has had an undercover job for the last two years."

Matt's eyes grow wide. "Like with the CIA?"

I can't help it, I roll my eyes. "No, honey, nothing like that." I wet my lips, giving myself time. "You know that guy you and Aaron had to help out of bed?"

"Yeah?" Matt cocks one eyebrow. "His girlfriend was all over Aaron."

Wait, he noticed something like that? Maybe he's more astute than I've given him credit for. Then I stiffen when I realize what he's said—Claudia, all over Aaron, in front of Jake, her really sweet fiancé—that she would do that when Jake was laid up. I sniff, like there's something moldy in the air. There is—Claudia. "Anyway, she was trying to tell you something about me being, uh, scantily clothed."

"Yeah, you explained it." Matt squeezes his eyes shut, trying to recall the conversation, I assume. "It was something about a party for the hospital."

I chew on my bottom lip and shoot a pleading glance to Ellen.

Ellen scoots her chair closer to Matt and takes his hand. "Sometimes, people have to go to extraordinary means to reach a goal." She massages an eyebrow. "Wait, let me start over." She clears her throat and her words come out in a rush. "What I'm trying to say is that Amy cleans houses in bikinis or French maid outfits, depending on what the client wants, so she can pay off her medical school loans."

Oh. My. God. She just blurted it out. I look at Matt. His eyes ping-pong from Ellen to me. He rubs a hand against the front of his shirt…over his heart. I ease closer to him on the couch. "You know how I never want to ask you or anyone else for money even though I know that Mark, Mike, and Luke can afford it?"

Matt nods slowly.

"It's always been extremely important for me to make my own way. You guys want to help me, I know that, but if you can imagine what it's like to be the only girl with five brothers ruling your life, you might be able to understand how I need to do this for myself. Yes, I used to clean houses in a bikini to make extra money, but none of the guys I cleaned for touched me or tried to get familiar. That was the main rule. They could watch, but touching was absolutely forbidden."

Matt's head flinches back slightly. I guess he's trying to reconcile his sweet little sister working at a job that must seem one fraction removed from a stripper. "You don't do it anymore?"

"Nope, I quit." I cross my fingers and sit on my hand. Matt doesn't need to know I've got one more gig to fulfill. "Please try to put yourself in my shoes. I wanted to be able to support myself. You guys have never asked anyone for a handout, and neither have I."

Matt scratches at his temple then he laughs. "I could never fit in your shoes." He shrugs. "And I could never make it through medical school." He pulls me in for a hug. I collapse on his big chest, but then have to pull back so I don't suffocate.

"Are you sure you're all right with this, big guy?" I ask.

"Long as you're not doing it anymore, I'm okay." He nods to Ellen. "But I wish you'd just have let us help you. If we all went in together, it wouldn't even pinch us to pay for your school."

I hug him tight then take his face in my hands. "I had to do it on my own, Matt." Tears well, but I blink them back. I know he only wants what's best for me. "But now that I've quit this job, I need you to promise me that you won't tell our brothers."

"Ah, heck, Amy, I've wanted to have a secret from those guys for years." He shrugs. "I know they've kept things from me because they think I'm not smart enough to understand stuff. Now I have my own secret."

I hug Matt. I complain a lot about my brothers, but today, I'm proud to be this bighearted fellow's little sister. I'll be thrilled if things work out for him and Ellen.

Someday, I hope I'll be as lucky in love, too.

Chapter Nine

Jake

I'm awakened from a fitful sleep by the chirp of my cell phone. I don't recognize the caller ID. My first thought is that Claudia has notified my law partners that I've embezzled from the firm. I haven't, of course, but I wouldn't put anything past her.

"Hello, this is Jake Sinclair," I answer tentatively.

"Oh, thank goodness I got you," a woman's voice shrieks.

I hold the phone away from my ear, shake my head then replace it. "Who is this?"

"It's Ellen Kurtz, Amy Maitland's friend. I'm worried about Amy." She sounds breathless, as if she's been running.

My heart races as my protective instincts kick in. "I'm probably the last person she'd want you to call, but what's up?"

"Since you ratted on her, you should know that she quit her fantasy maid job. But Rex, her boss, asked her to see one last client and I have a really bad feeling about it. I've always had premonitions and this one isn't good."

I scrub a hand across my eyes. "Do you think she's in danger?" My ribs don't hurt as much as usual as I ease myself to a sitting position. That's what adrenalin can do for you.

"Oh, geez, I hope not. She won't listen to me and I thought you might want to do something to redeem yourself. I can't ask anyone else because you're the only one besides me who knows about her job. Wait a minute, let me amend that. I know, you know, the chief of staff knows, and now her brother, Matt knows, thank you very much. He's promised not to tell his and Amy's other brothers but, bless his heart, he might accidently blab—especially if he knew about this last gig of hers. God knows what he'd do."

I'm fully awake now. "I'd love to do something for Amy. I wasn't the one who ratted on her."

"Yeah, I kind of figured it was that fiancée of yours, but why didn't you tell Amy the truth?"

"I don't know. As angry as I was at Claudia, I didn't want to replace one rat out for another, and I figured the damage had been done. Is Amy all right?"

"Well, she's mad as a hornet, but you're not the primary target anymore. In fact, I probably shouldn't tell you this, but underneath her anger, I think she still likes you."

"Really? Like I might have a chance?"

"I wouldn't get ahead of myself. The main thing is that the 'big reveal' hasn't caused any long term issues with her career at the hospital or as a doctor."

Thank God for that. "What can I do?" I'll do anything.

"Her client tonight is in a bad part of town, and I mean the worst. Can you show up at her gig and intercede? I'm working, or I'd go there myself."

I'm not supposed to drive for two weeks at least, but I say, "Absolutely, I'll go. When and where?"

Once I have the information from Ellen, I assure her I'll be there then say goodbye before I realize that, oh, shit, I don't even have a car. It was totaled in the accident. I'll need to take a cab to Kennedy Boulevard.

• • •

Amy

I finger my rosary beads with one hand as I pull into the dilapidated apartment complex. I realize Ellen was correct: this really is a bad part of town. But Rex has always made double and triple sure the clients are all right, and I've learned to trust his judgment, so upward and onward. It's only two hours then I'll be finished as a fantasy maid for good. I tell myself that no matter what the building looks like, Rex vetted this client the way he has all the others. So, it'll be fine.

Passing an overloaded dumpster, I gag at the odor of garbage and stale alcohol. Ew.

I'm checking the buildings for numbers. I'm way in the back of the complex before I find Building Twelve. A dog chained to an upstairs railing regards me balefully but doesn't bark. He's probably seen more threatening intruders.

There must be fifteen or more two story buildings on this lot and they've all seen better days—like in the 1960s. Mold and mildew creep up the concrete block walls and weeds have long since overtaken any landscaping.

I find Apartment Twelve F, where a battered Christmas wreath adorns the front door. I pull into a parking space in front and a scrawny cat peeks at me from behind a weed tree. Yes, weeds can grow into trees.

Ellen wasn't happy about me doing this last job and I'm sharing her sentiments as I turn off the ignition and grab my backpack. But everything Ellen said about this area and the looks of this place hit me all of a sudden, and I can't make myself get out of the car. I'm suddenly petrified that Rex goofed and I might be in a bad spot. I close my eyes and rest my forehead on the steering wheel, which reminds me of the steering wheel that crunched Jake's ribs, which reminds me of Jake, the cad, which brings that bitch Claudia to mind, which causes a growl of fury to swell in my chest.

Okay, that does it. Nothing like a jolt of anger to rouse some courage. I'd just opened the car door to swing my legs out when a taxi comes careening around the corner and parks in the space next to me. Someone's waving his arms in the backseat. I look closer through the tinted glass. Oh, for pity's sake, it's Jake. My heart races and I want to slap it still.

The back door of the taxi swings open. "Thank goodness I caught you," Jake says.

"What are you doing here?" I'm kind of screaming, mostly because I'm glad to see him, which is super annoying, especially when he shouldn't be out and about. "You should be home in bed." Okay, my first thought is for his wellbeing, but I put that down to my being his doctor. Aside from that, he's scum—which leads me to my second thought, "Leave me alone!" I toss my hair and make a beeline for the Christmas wreath.

"Don't knock on that door." Jake sounds hysterical.

I turn. "How did you know where I was?" I narrow my eyes at him. I don't want to look at him at all, but at least this way, he's blurred.

"Ellen called me. She had a premonition about this address and said you might be in danger." Jake grimaces as he eases his legs out of the taxi.

"You don't know Ellen well enough to listen to her premonitions," I snap at him. "Not to mention she's been known to be off base." Well, I hedge to myself, not often.

"That'll be eighteen-fifty," Jake's cab driver says.

"Just keep the meter running," Jake answers. "This might take a while." He holds on to the doorframe as he pulls himself up. I can tell he's hurting. I have to stop myself from helping him, but if he hadn't listened to worry wart Ellen, he'd be home in bed where he should be.

I decide I'm going to kill Ellen the next time I see her.

"Oh, no, it won't," I say, "because you're leaving."

"Not until you hear me out."

"Haven't you done enough harm already? You jeopardized not only my residency at the hospital, but potentially could have sabotaged my entire career. You cost me a good paying job where

I've never been in danger, and because your *girlfriend* had to tell my brother that I work naked, well, I can't even begin to tell you how low I think that is." I'm about to hyperventilate. Just saying the word *girlfriend* made me want to spit. I'm tapping my tennis shoe on the pavement. Real tough, Amy. I should be wearing combat boots.

"I wanted you to know that I wasn't the one who snitched on you."

"You came out here to tell me that?" I step forward and poke him in the arm...hard. I was headed for his chest, but I regrouped at the last second. I'm mad, but I couldn't be that mean. He winces. Good! "For a lawyer, that's a piss-poor opening statement."

He offers me half a shrug. "I also wanted to thank you for making me realize what a colossal mistake I was about to make."

"I have no clue what you're talking about." No, I'm not dense. I hope he's talking about breaking up with Claudia, but I don't want to jump to conclusions.

"I'm not getting married, at least, not to Claudia."

"Is there a reason I should care about that?" My heart pounds like a jackhammer again, but I contemplate the clouds like I'm bored.

"I hope so."

I'm mulling over what he means, what I hope he means, when I hear a jingling noise, like a bunch of tiny bells. It's the Christmas wreath. Someone has disturbed its solace. The door opens.

The guy standing in the doorway isn't green, but every other attribute mimics the Incredible Hulk, Lou Ferrigno version. Wild hair tops a face loaded with features that are too large—eyes, nose, mouth, and especially a forehead shelf that you could stand under to shield yourself from the rain. His eyebrows are like dense forests above his dark eyes.

The Hulk is topless, with b-cup man titties. I glance further down his considerable girth. He's wearing a loincloth and gladiator sandals, laced to the knees. I'll bet he has imprints on his calves when he takes them off.

For a moment, we all stand frozen. The taxi driver rolls up his window.

"You're late." The Hulk sounds like he has a throat full of gravel…with a Russian accent. I'm reminded of those very nasty Russian mafia guys who are into human trafficking.

"I'm, uh…" That would be 'speechless,' Amy. I wasn't really scared until I heard his voice. I'm getting woozy.

"Sorry, but she won't be cleaning your apartment today." Jake puts his arm around my shoulders. "She has a communicable disease and I need to remove her from the service. I'll be happy to find a substitute for you."

"If what she's got is catching, why are you so close to her?" The Hulk raises his eyebrow shelf.

"It can only be transmitted through sexual contact. She got it from me," Jake says.

I look at him sideways. He raises an eyebrow and nods, no doubt the expression he intimidates jurors with.

"Hey, I wasn't gonna touch her." The Hulk throws up his gorilla hands and backs away. "The guy on the phone said there's no touching allowed, so I just figured I'd sit and pant." He laughs at his cleverness. Ew. He'd probably be massaging himself under that loincloth.

"Yes, I'm sure you're an honorable man," Jakes says with a cough, "and you wouldn't dream of violating any rules. But my concern is for the girls, and this one," he nods at me gravely, "should be sidelined, at least temporarily."

Internally, I'm cracking up, but I maintain my cool. "Yes, I'm really sorry. I shouldn't have come." I wiggle around a bit. "The itching is driving me mad."

Now the Hulk has his hand on the doorknob. "I should have known this wouldn't work out. Things that sound too good to be true usually are."

"Tell you what," Jake says, "I'll send you a consolation prize. How about a DVD of *Gladiator* with Russell Crowe?"

I clamp a hand over my mouth to stifle a laugh.

"No, that's okay, but make sure you send me a credit on my Visa. And you can add a few bucks for my trouble. I don't dress like this every day." He backs into his apartment and slams the door.

Jake and I smile at each other when we hear the firm click of the deadbolt, and then he balls his fists.

"I have a mind to shut that boss of yours down," he says. "I can't believe he sent you to a place like this and a client like that." Jake stabs a thumb at the Christmas wreath, and then he shakes his head. "If anything happened to you…"

"Don't be too hard on Rex. He doesn't know all the neighborhoods and even though the client was creepy, he didn't have a criminal record or a history of violence against women." I shudder at the thought. "Rex would have checked for that. And besides, I could have told Rex about the neighborhood when Ellen first mentioned it was more than a tad sketchy, but I didn't. So really, I was the short-sighted one."

We stare at each other. I should probably drag this out, make him sweat, but I've never been good at playing hard-to-get. "You were saying before we were so rudely interrupted?" I ask.

"Ah, yes. I was getting ready to say that I couldn't marry Claudia not only after what she did, but because I found myself falling for someone else."

"Oh." I hold my breath and make myself stand ramrod still so I won't ruin everything by attacking him right here.

"That someone is you."

I exhale. I feel a case of happy feet smoldering in my tennies. "I see. Is that your closing statement?"

He steps closer, and I see his hands twitch as though he'd really like to touch me. "No, Amy, it's just the beginning."

"And you assume that's information I want to hear?" That's the best hard-to-get statement I can muster as I find myself stepping toward him, too.

"As I said before, I hope so."

"Well, you'd be right." I grin. I want to let out a hoot, but the Hulk might hear. "Ordinarily, this is the part where the hero sweeps the heroine into his arms."

"Sorry, but the sweeping will have to wait." Jake looks down at me. "However, my lips are fair game."

I stand on tiptoes and take his face in my hands—gently because I don't want to do anything that might delay his ribs healing. As soon as I can, I want to take "gentle" out of this equation and focus on making my fantasies of this wonderful man real. "Jake Sinclair, you are one hell of a lawyer."

He smiles. "Amy Maitland, you are one hell of a fantasy, maid or not."

He closes his lips on mine.

Chapter Ten

Amy, Six Weeks Later

Woo hoo, Jake's ribs have healed. The Hulk incident slowed the process a bit. He shouldn't have been out and about, much less ready to do battle, but of course, I'm thrilled he showed up to rescue me.

He declared himself one hundred percent a week ago, but I insisted we wait an additional week before we jump each other's bones.

I've been dreaming of this day—or more to the point, I've been aching for it. While Jake has regained his strength, we've strolled around Lake Osceola, gone to movies, and introduced each other to favorite haunts like Fleet Peeples Park and New Smyrna Beach. I'm more impressed with him every day. He's shared his hopes and dreams with me and, most importantly, I've learned that he spells integrity with a capital "I." It's how he lives his life.

I have to admit that introducing Jake to my brothers was a little intense—for me, if not them. I wasn't sure they'd ever relinquish their protectiveness toward me, but they seemed to feel that Jake was up to taking over that task. Phew. Matt paved the way with the siblings. Matt's intelligence quotient may be subpar, but his emotional quotient is through the roof. I wonder how he ever passed his fireman exams. He must have lived on FireQuiz.com. Well, he's nothing if not determined. He and Ellen are doing great. They're making their own story.

Meanwhile, I've got an outfit to ponder for my big night with Jake—as in do I dress as the French maid or just wear the bikini? It's only fitting that we consummate the new direction of our relationship the way we started it.

I spread the pieces of my French maid outfit over the bed, feather duster and all. That clinches my decision. I imagine tickling Jakes' naked torso…and his sex…with the duster. Just the notion of an elevation in his manhood has me fanning myself.

Okay, here's the outfit: black bustier with white lace trim and fake lace stays, a ruffled thong for the bottom half, thigh high fishnet hose with little bows at the top, a tiny red, heart-shaped apron that reads "At Your Service," and to top it off, a black satin ribbon to tie around my neck.

I smile as I pick up the bustier and begin fastening the hooks in front. The built-in, pushup bra isn't necessary and when I wore it for cleaning, I had to be extra careful not to spill out the top. With Jake, I'll just spill away. When I'm as dressed as I can be in an outfit that emphasizes nakedness, I slip on my trench coat, grab my car keys, and stick the feather duster in my deep pocket, feathers up.

Then I scoot out the door.

Jake's expecting me at his apartment at seven. He's making some dish from *Mastering the Art of French Cooking.* That's another thing I've just learned about him. He likes to cook. Instead of tackling the monumental task of cooking his way through the whole book in a year, like in *Julie & Julia,* he's doing one recipe a month. I'm the happy guinea pig. And how appropriate that the recipes are French!

My heart's thrumming like the plucked strings of a guitar when Jake opens his front door. He pulls me into his arms and nuzzles my ear. Then he holds me at arm's length.

"Is there rain in the forecast?" He peers out the door to the clear blue sky. "Why the trench coat?"

I ease past him and stop in the center of the living room and turn. "You said you were cooking French tonight, right?" I begin to unbelt my coat.

"Uh, yeah?" His voice rises on the second word.

"I thought a little French preamble might heighten the effect. You know what they say about gourmet cooking, it's half about the food and the other half is presentation." I slowly open my coat to unveil the full panoply of French maidery.

Jake coughs, and I notice the front of his pants start to tent. It's nice to know I have *all* of his attention.

I close the space between us and run my hands up his hard chest and then down over his waist where I place my open palm lightly over the bulge behind his zipper. The bulge grows and nudges my hand. "Just consider me the aperitif."

He drags in a breath and manages, "No, Amy, you're all five courses."

His eyes grow dark and he sweeps me into his arms. As a doctor, I want to protest that while his ribs have knitted, he shouldn't overdo it. But tonight, I'm not a doctor. I'm a fantasy maid. And I'm already tingling all over. When Jake ducks his head and slides his tongue along my dangerously pushed-up breasts and into my cleavage, I swallow and feel myself start to pant. Now I fully understand the old romance novel cliché, 'heaving bosoms,' because mine are clearly straining to spill out of my bustier and capture both his undivided attention and his mouth. Lovely aromas of wine and herbs are wafting from the kitchen, but my gastric juices have migrated south. I'm focused on the chef; his erotic, all-male scent is making my temperature rise. Right now, I don't care if I ever eat again.

Jake puts me down and taps my nose. His slow smile and the fingertip he runs along the ruffled edge of my bustier tell me he knows exactly what I need. "Let me put the kitchen on simmer."

"Simmer's good." My voice sounds hoarse. I'm about to boil over and he's barely touched me. I want him to feel the same way.

I slither up behind him and slide my hands around his waist and down his thighs while he turns down the heat...in the kitchen. He stills. I guess he's trying to concentrate on what he's doing, but he betrays himself when his breath hitches, and his gorgeous butt snugs tight into my belly. I feel the pound of his heart against my face when I lean against his back. He's wearing a tight, sky blue t-shirt and jeans that look like they've been washed a thousand times. And he's barefoot. I love the anatomy of the foot and Jake has great feet. His toes are evenly graduated from the pinky up and the tendons in his feet rope sinuously up to his shapely ankles. I guess most girls don't get off on feet. I'm not enamored of sucking on toes or any of that foot fetish stuff, but the instrument of human propulsion can be a beautiful sight to behold. And then my eyes travel up.

Jake removes my hands from his anatomy and pushes out of my embrace. He turns from the stove and catches my gaze. I'm sure my nostrils have flared, taking in the musky scent of him. I want nothing more than to tear down the zipper on his jeans, release his cock, and have my way with him. The stuttering rise and fall of his chest and his hooded eyes make me realize how much he'd like to unfetter and plunder my imprisoned parts, as well. Will we ever make it to the bedroom?

He points in that direction. I want to sprint, but I purse my lips and say, "Oui, monsieur." I extract the feather duster from my pocket, shimmy off the trench coat, and tiptoe to the bedroom in my ballet flats. They're the one practical accoutrement to this ridiculous outfit. Some of the girls work in high heels, but I can't risk an injury. When I enter Jake's bedroom, I start dusting his chest of drawers as though I'm only there to get some cleaning done. I whistle La Marseillaise.

I'm dusting away, though not stirring up anything until Jake's hands encircle my waist and pull me back against his strong chest. I close my eyes as he spreads his fingers across my abdomen. I hold my breath when one hand migrates north and one heads south. Cripes. I sneeze. Surely there's a physiological reason why I sneeze when I get turned on. Making a quick mental note to look it up in my Guyton & Hall Textbook, I switch off the analytical doctor and happily morph into the all-for-pleasure fantasy maid. Except the man I'm leaning against isn't a fantasy. He's very real and right as rain. I feel him shudder behind me at the same time his still restrained erection prods the cleft of my buttocks. "Are you cold?" I ask.

"Anything but." He chuckles. "I guess I'm nervous."

Okay, so am I. If I let myself think too hard about how much I care about this man, I'll dissolve in a pool of jitters. Better concentrate on my fantasy persona.

I turn in Jake's arms, not losing body contact as I rub against him on my merry way. Looking into his glorious green eyes, I say, "Voulez vous coucher avec moi, ce soir?"

His lips turn up in a half-grin. "Was there ever any doubt?"

And then his eyes darken, and he slides his northbound hand up over my captive breasts to the velvet bow at my throat. Maybe he's had enough of my fantasy maid shtick…and not enough Amy. I'm all for that.

He gently tugs at the ribbon around my neck then stops. "I think I'll save that for last," he says, moving to the stays on my bustier. I suck in a breath to make the corset easier to unhook. His fingers glide over the center of my chest as my confined nipples inch toward freedom and finally spill loose. I'm momentarily disappointed when he sucks in a hard breath at the sight of my distended areolas but proceeds to ignore them. He deftly moves his hands down my torso and my disappointment is supplanted by the heat liquefying between my thighs. When he unhooks the last stay, the corset flops to the floor. I let out my breath and almost collapse with it, but then Jake's hands find my breasts. I close my eyes as he thumbs both nipples into points that are so hard and tight I lose all sense of time and place. My knees start to shake.

I need his mouth on me *now*.

He grasps me by the shoulders. "Amy." I look up into his eyes. He seems to be drinking me in. "Making love to you means the world to me." His lip twitches a bit and I press a finger to it. "That's the sweetest thing anyone's ever said to me."

He picks me up and carries me to the bed. I kick off my ballet flats on the way. I'm worried about him carting so much weight, but he's not huffing or acting like I weigh more than a five pound sack of flour. I feel cherished in his arms and when he gently places me on the bed I know I'm no sack of flour to him.

He starts on my legs, slowly peeling down the fishnet thigh highs, stopping to massage and kiss the backs of my knees. I find this inordinately sexy. When he gets to my feet, he tosses the hose off, sits on the bed, and puts my feet in his lap. "You work so hard at the hospital," he says, kneading my calves. I close my eyes and melt into the sensation of his strong fingers on my muscles. I breathe deeply, getting a delightful whiff of his sandalwood soap, enhanced by his warm skin.

And then he starts working his hands back up my legs. My breath catches as his thumbs graze the inside of my thighs. He eases one thumb under my thong and fireworks explode. I arch my back and grind into his probing fingers. My "At Your Service" apron has never been more appropriate, though I yank at the tie to pull it off as Jake peels down my lace thong. Except for the ribbon around my neck, I am completely naked...and Jake has far too many clothes on. Evidently, he just noticed the same thing because he springs off the bed and throws off his t-shirt. He unzips his jeans and lets them fall. He's commando. I guess he was anticipating this. I smile at his erect penis like I'm five years old and have just been handed the most luscious lollipop ever created. In a little while, I'll get to lick and suck on that lollipop. "Wow," I hear myself say. "That's the most beautiful appendage I've ever seen. No listing to the left or right and perfectly formed." I prop myself on my elbows for a better look.

Jake throws his head back and laughs. He makes no attempt to cover up his object of desire. No embarrassment there. "Thanks, Doc. It's a bit out of practice."

"Doesn't look like it needs any priming." I sit up and slide a hand down the glorious length. It answers my touch by pushing into the fold of my palm around it as I stroke its taut silkiness.

Jake moans and I cup his balls and gently pull him closer…to my mouth. This is not something I've ever craved—until now. All I want is to give him pleasure. I nibble up and down his length then stop to suck ever so gently on the tip. He tastes like the ocean, fresh and slightly salty. I take him deep in my throat and shudder as he throbs there. I begin to suck harder.

"Amy, please," he groans, "what you're doing is incredible, but I can't last like this and I don't want to come yet."

I feel his hands on my head. I want to keep licking and pulling on his heavy arousal, but he strokes my eyebrows and I disengage to look up at him. The look in his eyes does it. I pull the end of the ribbon at my neck, hand it to him, and lay back on the bed. My heart is pounding and I swear my vagina is clenching. It's that anxious to be filled by this spectacular man. "Don't even think about doing anything but getting inside me," I say. "I'm so hot for you, I may explode."

Jake chuckles, but he's not into taking instruction, at least not now. "Amy, I've been thinking about sucking on your breasts since the night I met you. Indulge me."

He kneels on the bed between my legs and hovers over me, teasing my thighs with his penis. I wrangle around and arch my back for his entry, but he has other ideas. He slips one hand under my thigh and anchors me there. Propped on his other elbow, he lowers his mouth to my breast and rolls his tongue around my hardened nipple and…Oh. My. Stars! My need is so intense that I start to buck on the bed. He tries to hold me still, but it's not an easy task. He's sucking hard now and I know if I touch myself, I'll be gone in one stroke. I need him inside me and this time I'm not taking no for an answer. I grab his penis firmly and guide him to my opening. He doesn't object. He leans over to pluck a condom packet from his bedside table. Just to make sure he's not going anywhere, I don't let go of his penis.

He stretches the condom over his shaft and when he slides inside me, I want to shout Hallelujah! He's so big, so warm, and so perfectly suited for the cozy space I'm providing. He moans in my ear then he pulls back to stare down at me.

"I love you, Amy."

"Yeah?" I feel the tears spilling down my cheeks. "Well, me too."

"I don't want to come right away, but you feel so damn good," he says. He thrusts deep and I hold him there so we can both catch our breaths. I hug him tight, thinking about the two of us as one, molded together perfectly. I rub one hand up and down his back, feeling his strong, knitted ribs. What if he hadn't had that auto accident? Would he have married Claudia? I shudder.

"What's wrong, Amy?" He brushes my wet cheeks with his knuckles as he looks down at me.

"Absolutely nothing," I say.

And then he starts to move in me, deeply thrusting in a slow rhythm and not taking his eyes from my face. "I want you to come with me."

I take his hand and guide it to my clitoris. "Just a little rub there should do the trick, but don't do it until you're right on the verge."

"Honey, I'm over the verge." He puts his fingers on my bud and my explosion begins. It starts with a spasm that grips me in waves; I shake from head to toe with the intensity of it. I want to burst with love for this man. And just as my climax subsides, his begins. He pulls me close and rocks me with his release, and I dissolve into tears.

He kisses my hair. "I thought this would be a happy occasion." He chuckles.

"I've never been happier." I sob.

"Does this mean you're going to cry down the aisle when we get married?"

What did he say? I didn't think my happiness could ramp up any higher, but my chest fills with warmth and a contentment I've never known. "I just might," I say. I wrap my arms around him. I'm never letting go.

More From This Author

(From *The Gettysburg Vampire*)

1863

The locomotive sped silently past Union Colonel Malcolm McClellan, whose blank stare belied his shock. No whistle pierced the air. No smoke billowed from the massive steam engine. No vibration shook the ground. A chill breeze had stirred the silence and set him gazing to the northeast through the mounting dusk. Otherwise, he would have missed the Stonewall Jackson altogether. Summer granted no chilling breezes. Malcolm looked down the line at his men, huddled behind the trees at their makeshift camp in northern Virginia.

"Did you see that, colonel?" Clayton asked, his voice as shaken as the air. "That sucker just busted on through. Didn't slow down a mite." The men had spent the previous night pulling up a large section of track. Any normal train would have ground to a halt or derailed.

"It didn't need to slow down, Clay," Malcolm said. "It seems to have levitated." Malcolm stared at the empty horizon where the train had sliced through at breakneck speed. His heart raced.

"Pardon me, colonel, but what does that mean?" Jack asked.

"I believe the train flew, gentlemen." Malcolm stooped and picked up a rock. He flung it in the direction the train had sped.

Jack collapsed to his knees. "Good Lord, colonel. I'd figure I was crazy if we hadn't all seen the same thing. We did all see the same thing?" He looked at his fellow soldiers, who all nodded. "You think that was the ghost train, colonel?"

Malcolm drew in a deep breath, and then blew it out with a cough. "I'm sure of it." He helped Jack to his feet. Rampant rumors of the ghost train had circulated for months, but actually seeing it had caught Malcolm unaware. His stomach churned.

"So, what do we do now, colonel?" Henry's voice squeaked. "Want William and me to mount up and follow the train?"

Malcolm removed his hat and wiped his brow with a handkerchief. "I don't believe you could catch it, not at the speed that train was traveling. Our orders from General Meade were to intercept the train, and since we can't derail it, I'd like to try to get on it. I think the only way to do that is to entice it to stop."

"What you think that train'll stop for, colonel? Dancing girls?" Jack chuckled nervously.

Malcolm narrowed his eyes. "No, Jack. I'm no expert on ghosts, but I imagine the only thing that can stop that train is death. If I had to guess, I'd say the Stonewall Jackson is some kind of latter-day death carriage collecting newly minted souls. And there are plenty of them these days on both sides of the conflict, though being a Confederate train, I doubt it would take kindly to our Yankee souls." Malcolm's men looked back at him with questioning stares.

"I hope you're not suggesting one of us volunteer to be a casualty, colonel." William glanced sideways at Malcolm.

"No, William, I'm suggesting we *pose* as casualties."

Again, all four men looked puzzled.

"This time tomorrow, we'll stage a scene right here where we tore up the tracks. We'll make it look like we were ambushed trying to fix the ties. Just William and me. We can smear some rabbit blood on our clothes and lie by the tracks. The rest of you can stand watch from behind the trees."

"In your blue uniforms, they'll know you're Union, colonel," Henry said. "Only Rebs would be trying to fix Confederate tracks."

"We won't be in uniform, Henry."

"Surely not just in your skivvies, colonel."

Malcolm smiled. "I'm afraid so." He patted the lieutenant's shoulder, and the churning in his stomach calmed as his plan coalesced.

"Then what, colonel?" William asked. "When they see we're not dead, what's to keep them from making it so?"

Malcolm squinted into the afternoon sun. "I don't know, William, but if they think we're Rebs, we shouldn't be in immediate danger." He half grinned. "You've been wounded before, haven't you, Lieutenant?"

"Yessir, at Antietam."

"So was I, at Gettysburg. I still have pain in my shoulder, and I've seen you favor your right leg. I believe we can seem wounded in a way that would fool the ghosts. From what little I know about them, ghosts aren't typically violent. They'll stop to pick up dead recruits, but I don't think they'd do us any harm once they see we're still alive."

"Colonel McClellan, sir, pardon me, but I think you're assuming a lot about the nature of ghosts, when you've never even met one."

"They were once people just like us, William. Follow my lead. I did Shakespeare at the Point." Malcolm smiled. "There's something about performing that frees a man."

"Pardon me, colonel, but I'm no actor. I'm not sure they'd believe me, sir." William removed his cap and twisted it in his hands. "I've never been a good liar, and I think they'd see right through me."

"Well, that should even the odds, William, since you'll be able to see right through them," Henry said. "You know, them being ghosts and all."

The men chuckled, and Malcolm nodded. "All right, then, William. If you feel you'd be a liability, join the other men. You can all be my audience."

"You sure you want to do this, colonel?" Henry asked. "I don't know how much help we can be. I mean, you can't shoot a ghost, right? They're already dead."

Malcolm looked to the northeast, where, he assumed, this time tomorrow, the train would again materialize. "If you've got a better idea, by all means speak up. But we don't have much time."

Malcolm turned from the tracks and headed back to their camp. He quickened his pace as the adrenalin pumped through his system and his plan took shape. He'd feign a head injury. That would make the most sense. He'd appear to be knocked out, and then he'd "regain consciousness" once he was aboard the train.

He thought back to his acting days at West Point. In his role as Shylock, he'd mastered the character of a miserly old moneylender. Surely he could play a wounded Confederate soldier. And if he said he was from Maryland, he wouldn't have to affect a Southern accent, though he might need to practice a rebel yell.

Though he'd been skeptical of the ghost train's existence, he couldn't deny what he and his men had just seen. Over the past year, the legend of the Stonewall Jackson had become fodder for local storytellers, and the tales swirling about the inhabitants of the train had escalated from ghosts to other more dreadful creatures like vampires. Malcolm had seen evidence of diaphanous spirits on the battlefield and felt the prickle of eerie presences. He could fathom the existence of ghosts. But vampires?

In the mood for more Crimson Romance?
Check out *As If You Never Left Me*
by Katriena Knights
at *CrimsonRomance.com*.

About the Author

Susan Blexrud divides her time between Orlando, Florida, and Asheville, North Carolina, where she leads two book clubs, advocates for gay youth, writes a monthly column for All Souls Cathedral, quilts, watches birds, cooks her way through *Mastering the Art of French Cooking*, and maintains a public relations consultancy. She's the mother of two grown children, and her constant writing companions are a Chihuahua named Baby and a cockatiel named Romeo. She has penned six novels. *His Fantasy Maid* is her second book for Crimson Romance, and she is hard at work on her next story, *Valentine Vote*.

www.ingramcontent.com/pod-product-compliance
Lightning Source LLC
Chambersburg PA
CBHW010644100726
47900CB00011B/2961